Clash of
EGOS

(A Novel)

by

Jude Berinyuy

Miraclaire
Publishing

First Published in 2022

Miraclaire Publishing
Kansas City, MO 64133, USA
www.miraclairepublishing.com / info@miraclairepublishing.com

ISBN-13: 978-1-954154-15-5
© 2022 Miraclaire Publishing / Jude Berinyuy

Printed in the United States of America

Miraclaire Publishing makes every effort to ensure the accuracy of all the information ("Content") in its publications. However, Miraclaire and its agents and licensors make no representations or warranties whatsoever as to the accuracy, completeness, or suitability for any purpose of the Content and disclaim all such representations and warranties, whether expressed or implied to the maximum extent permitted by law. Any views expressed in this publication are the views of the author and are not necessarily the views of Miraclaire.

Dedication

To all troubleshooters and those with tamed egos

CHAPTER ONE

The population that turned out to welcome the heroes of that epic trek was a mammoth one. As early as dawn, they started gathering at the junction where three roads from their respective villages met. They wanted to see for themselves whether their rulers had been healed of their ailments before believing it. The mammoth crowd had been hanging around that junction to the sacred fountain for several hours and nothing seemed to be happening. They had been informed the previous day that the delegation to Nkim would arrive first thing the next morning. Now the sun was overhead and yet the old, the young as well as mothers and children, with anxious faces, resisted the scorching sun apparently ready to exercise undetermined patience to the end. From all indications, not even a child wanted to be told the story that definitely was going to be one in a lifetime. They really had to see with their two eyes before believing that the long-lasting rivalry between descendants of Tikak clan had actually come to an end and their leaders had recovered from their bad shape!

It was in the midst of that historic crowd that Wiymanla spotted someone like his wife. At first, he did not believe his eyes. He rubbed his eyes with the back of his hand, unconsciously moving towards the direction where the lady stood. Some ten metres from the spot, Wiymanla stopped and observed again. Yes! It was true! That was his wife he had not seen for over a year now. The last time he saw her was that night when his late father left Nos Baptist Hospital never to be seen again. There, she stood discussing and smiling with Fonkwa, their neighbour in the village. She was very relaxed and seemed to be less concerned with the busy atmosphere at the junction. The man was carrying a new-born baby on his arms, feeling very free. Wiymanla felt his adrenaline rising at a geometric rate. He began breathing faster and harder too, fuming with anger at the same time. He thought of moving straight to where those two stood and confronting them right away. In fact, he wanted to punch someone on the face before his temper could subside. He looked round and realised that nobody had noticed him, not even his wife and Fonkwa who remained stationed where he had first spotted them, apparently unperturbed. Wiymanla quickly readjusted and restrained, trying to compose himself. He had suddenly realised that he was beginning to act like someone insane and that that was neither the right place nor the right time to pose such a bestial act. He left instantly for Kou, his native village, for fear that his continuous stay there could make him lose control of himself and act irrationally.

What provoked the gathering at the junction had come a long way, leaving behind countless number of casualties along the path. For more than half a century, there had existed cold war among the people of Nos, Membia and Kou which sometimes led to open confrontation. The rivalry stemmed from a number of issues but the most prominent was the fight for supremacy. In the past, the three fondoms had lived together happily and harmoniously like the true descendants of the Tikak clan. Their communal lifestyle and understanding made it difficult for an outsider to identify someone to a particular fondom. Only people from the clan were able to know whether someone was from Nos, Membia or Kou because they had a unique way of talking that was peculiar to each fondom. The unity that flourished in the veins of sons and daughters of this clan attracted a lot of jealousy and envy from the neighbouring tribes. They tried to instil that type of oneness in their own land but failed woefully.

With the passage of time, as the older generation of Tikak clan faded out, so too were those values that had kept the people intact. A much more enthusiastic, less conservative and vulgar generation was gradually installing itself in the land. Although the people of the clan still functioned as an entity, there were already signs that the cords that had held them together for so many years were already weakened. Once in a while, misunderstanding, especially over land issue, crept up between the inhabitants of the three fondoms. This was however managed tactfully and immediately by the Fons and their closest subjects before it degenerated. They were largely made up of the last surviving species of those who migrated from Tikak to the present settlement, close to a century ago. Throughout the existence of the older generation, it was unheard of that any of the three tribes had an open conflict with one another.

When the last survivors of the migrated Tikak clan eventually got extinct following the deaths of venerated Fons of Nos, Membia and Kou, alongside their subjects, a fissure was created that finally opened on the wall for envious politicians from other tribes to have easy access into the minds of the youths of the clan. Through manoeuvre, they succeeded to

3

lure the successors of the late Fons into politics who joined different political parties based on their aspirations. The Fon of Nos opted for the ruling party and within a short period of time, it propelled him to the top. He began having clashes of ideologies with his colleagues which led to disagreements between them over major issues that concerned the land. This did not stop the Fon of Nos from pursuing his political ambitions. Instead, it made him more popular among his people as well as among other Fons from the neighbouring tribes. His hunger for power grew in leaps and bounds every passing day.

Before the Fon of Membia and that of Kou could open their eyes to embrace the political vision of the party in power, the Fon of Nos had imposed himself as the number one man from the Tikak clan and was now simply referred to as the "paramount ruler of Tikak clan" by many people. This appellation was promoted by the sons and daughters of Nos fondom. Even other small Fons under Nos fondom preferred to refer to His Royal Highness as the supreme ruler of Tikak clan. The Fon of Membia and that of Kou were very uncomfortable with that, and it further widened the gap between the three. They could no longer come together and carry out some obligatory rituals and sacrifices in the land as they used to do in the past. Discrimination became strongly rooted in the land and the communal life style that had existed between the people of Nos, Membia and Kou was all gone. Each fondom was now concerned with the well-being of its people.

Meanwhile, the Fon of Nos continued to excel in politics. He took another gigantic step when he skilfully worked his way

4

into the Fons' Union (FU) for the entire Region and was made the Secretary General. This meant that he now belonged to the circle of those who, by the powers vested on them by tradition, had the unconditional right to decide on how the affairs of the land had to be run. For so many years, the union was a selfless one as it strictly functioned on the motto: *we are servants and not masters*. The leaders worked for the interest of cultural preservation and promotion. FU stood out in the entire country as an exemplary association. It made sure that cultural aspects that were dangerous to human existence were dropped. The Head of State was fond of constantly using the union as a reference for the citizens. He kept on stressing that through cultural preservation and promotion, FU had demonstrated that the country now had something it could take to the global table and there, it would be seen there too as a giver and not just a taker.

As time went on the union that was originally apolitical started drifting away from the original course. The dense political wind of change that was blowing over the country swept them off their feet. Fons joined politics and soaked themselves in it to the marrow. They started eyeing juicy posts in the government. This divided the union into political and apolitical members. Even with the first group, there were those of the ruling party and opposition. Each Fon dragged his people along and those who refused to follow the footsteps of their leader became enemies. They suffered the consequences as the ruler made sure that any decision in the land in which those recalcitrant fellows were directly or indirectly involved worked in their disfavour. The comprehension and unity that had reigned among the Fons for so many years was subsequently destroyed by vaulting ambition and power struggle. The common slogan among the members of the union became: *politics na njangi, you scratch my back I scratch your back.* In whatever decision the leaders took, the Fons considered what they stood to benefit. State grants for the running of the union were siphoned by few individuals and kept in personal accounts. Most of the Fons became hypnotised as they allowed themselves to be consumed by the spirit of slandering, betrayal and backbiting. The Fons' union that had stood the test of time was thus rocked and wrecked until it finally collapsed and ceased to exist!

CHAPTER TWO

Some years ago, His Royal Highness, the Fon of Nkim, had had to intervene and lay to rest a leadership crisis that once crept up between the Fons of Nos, Membia and Kou. The crisis stemmed from a dispute over a piece of land that stretched into River Mairin, along the boundary separating the three fondoms. The peninsular had never actually belonged to somebody. Inhabitants from any part of the clan went there whenever they wanted and fished without any problem. Each of the three Fons once in a while went there to commune with the gods of the land. One day, it so happened that they met at that piece of land simultaneously and there was an unprecedented clash that almost resulted into inter-tribal war. They had each come to offer their usual individual sacrifices to the gods and none of them had imagined that he would meet the others there.

In the history of the clan, a joint sacrifice had never been made on that land since the settlement of the three fondoms on the present site. The unplanned meeting between these leaders was certainly not an occasion to do what had evidently not been sanctioned by the gods. There was therefore need for one of the three Fons to be allowed to start first while the others loitered around waiting for their individual turn. Nobody wanted to second the other as they all claimed to have undisputed right over the piece of land. The Fon of Kou stood firm that he had to start because he had ruled longer than the other two. His point was immediately dismissed as null and invalid by the Fon of Nos who reminded his colleagues that he was the eldest and by virtue of his age, he had to commence. As the Benjamin among the three, the Fon of Membia was in a weaker position but refused to give in and kept on insisting that he was the first to arrive. On that day, no sacrifice was made and the three Fons eventually had to return to their various fondoms without a compromise.

When His Royal Highness, the Fon of Nkim heard of the stalemate, he summoned the three Fons for what turned out to be a sermon of one speaker. In his speech, the Fon of Nkim admitted that misunderstanding between what he called *children of a common parentage* was unavoidable because Nos, Membia and Kou were individuals in their own right with different character traits. For that reason, misunderstanding was bound to occasionally show its ugly face because that is what leads to understanding each other better. He added rather jokingly that it was better to live with a devil one knew than with an angel that one knew nothing of. His Royal Highness however condemned the misunderstanding that stemmed from what he called *power struggle*. He reminded the three Fons that in every home there was always one who was given birth to first, even in the case of twins! By virtue of that natural phenomenon called birth, the law of nature must not be abused. He nonetheless emphasised that to be first born was neither a reason for a person to walk on his siblings nor to claim that he was their leader. Mutual respect for one another was what the Fon of Nkim laid emphasis on. In the course of the speech, the three Fons nodded ceaselessly visibly satisfied. Each of them definitely knew where he belonged and realised where he had gone wrong. Nobody needed to remind them who the first or last born was. They knew it by instinct and even physically, the writing was clearly written on the wall. By the time the Fon of Nkim finished his sermon, the three Fons got up and embraced each other with a lot of remorse, visibly resolved never to allow themselves to be controlled by irrational reasoning again.

Just few years after, the Fons of Nos, Membia and Kou were at each other's throat again. This time around, the tension was engineered by the publication of an almanac ranking the Fons of the clan. On that publication, *Nos Forum Magazine* brandished His Royal Highness, the Fon of Nos, as the paramount ruler of the clan. In this biannual edition, his picture was conspicuously projected in a unique poster that carried other Fons in minimised characters. He wore a traditional cap from which hung out *Njongsekigum*, which crowded it like feathers of a hen on incubation. His Royal Highness looked very composed in his sitting posture and kept a smile that immediately communicated his inner feelings. On both sides of him, and in very reduced sizes, stood the Fons of Membia and Kou wearing plain traditional caps. They were also smiling but their overall facial expressions betrayed them. They seemed to be smiling in spite of themselves! Just slightly below them, there was a series of third class chiefs who littered the greater part of the poster in a disorderly manner, each with a posture that begged for clearer visibility!

Although the Fons of Membia and Kou tried to resist the urge to publicly express their disgruntlement against what they saw as a slap on their face, it was difficult to be indifferent. The publication was indeed a big blow to their personalities. They wondered who must have conspired with the publisher of *Nos Forum* to render them figure heads, not more than second class chiefs of the clan. That was in fact an attempt to push them to the background and project the Fon of Nos as the supreme ruler of the clan! Perhaps they might have taken it with a pinch of salt but the speculations that it was a ploy perpetrated by the Fon of Nos, made the other two Fons to fume with uncontrolled anger. They condemned what they called political manoeuvre from hierarchy and incited their people to rise against misrepresentation of facts. In reality, the Fons of Membia and Kou did not contest the paramountcy of their colleague. Their problem was that it had been abused on the almanac. He was paramount in Nos fondom that comprised many sub chiefs like the Fons of Kiluum, Ndzeem, Ndzerem, Ngashom, Nkan, Njoh, Jav, Joro and Gwan who were disseminated over all his fondom, just like the Fons of Membia and Kou were paramount in their own fondoms. The only difference was that the Fon of Nos had quite a good number of sub chiefs under him unlike his colleagues that had just a handful of them.

The people of Nos wanted to take advantage of the fact that their fondom was the largest in terms of land and population in the entire clan to crush and bring Membia and Kou under him. Nos had a very vast piece of land and a population that could compete for numerical supremacy with any other clan in the entire Region. The steady growth in her population was due to the strategy of the then ruler who led the people in the days of migration. Since the Tikak clan was the first to find a larger and convenient site for settlement, the Fon of Nos embraced every minority group that came after and settled in

10

his own part of the land. The people had to pay allegiance and regard him as their leader. This was contrarily to the conservatism practised in Membia and Kou. The then leaders of the two tribes put in place a system that kept away strangers from their land. They made their people to understand that it was dangerous to accept migrants who did not share the same cultural values with them. Besides, it had taken them too long to find the present site and they were not ready to lose it one day to other group all in the name of hospitality.

The influx of different groups of people to Nos made the fondom to grow exponentially. Even in terms of development, Nos surpassed Membia and Kou by far. It was regarded as the second most developed area after Damenda, the headquarters of the Region. The people of Membia and Kou knew and admitted all this but categorically refused that those factors could be used by the people of Nos to usurp them. Judging from the way these two tribes fiercely stood their grounds as independent fondoms, the publication had come to fuel up the tension that was already visible among the three tribes. The disgruntlement and protest of the two Fons went on in the background. The Fon of Nos remained calm but unshakable. He stood his grounds as the paramount ruler and made sure that he was seen as such in all aspects. His people supported him with all their might and took it upon themselves to make sure that the appellation stood and spread as far as possible. This made the relationship between the three tribes further tense.

The tension that went on for years and seemed to have no end finally reached its climax and exploded when Wiymanla's father was brutally killed and his remains dumped at the boundary between Nos and Kou. The protest against the macabre incident that all began like a child's play and eventually degenerated into an inter-tribal war between Nos on one hand and Kou and Membia on the other. Immediately Wiymanla's father's body was found, the people of Kou reacted almost instantly. The following morning, they arrested a palm wine tapper from Nos and tortured him to death. They also set ablaze the *clando* that was carrying food stuff from Kou to Nos. The driver was alone inside and was burnt to ashes. Upon hearing this, the people of Nos also reacted promptly and struck back immediately.

His Royal Highness, the Fon of Nos summoned some elders of the land in his palace The gathering which took place around 10pm was an unprecedented one. First of all, the timing was very unusual. The Fon gave instructions that only those who lived nearer to the palace should be involved because it would take too much time if everyone who mattered had to be part of the meeting. According to him, things were getting out of hand and he could not wait at all because all eyes were on him to do something. When the elders received *toi fon* that they were needed in the palace that night, they were not happy at all. They wondered what it was that could not wait till morning. They grumbled as they got out of bed, struggling to situate the position of their staffs in that exceptionally dark night. Had it not been that this was from the supreme ruler of the land, most of them would not have respected the summons. The lone item on agenda was the unexpected attack perpetrated on them by their brothers from Kou, and the pending war on the clan. He also wanted to make known his position and to seek for advice on the issue.

As soon as the elders filed entered and took their positions at the meeting ground, His Royal Highness did not wait for any other formalities. He cleared his throat and went straight to the crux of the matter:

"I must first start by apologizing for stealing you out of your beds so late into the night. Our people say when you see a toad in broad daylight, either it is pursuing something or something is pursuing it. If I have summoned this emergency meeting, it is because something is pursuing us. The people of Kou have struck and the effect is already being felt by our wives and children. I do not know what should be done. Should we strike back or should we go in for peaceful negotiation?"

Elder Ndzev got up and lackadaisically performed the greeting rituals that were due His Royal Highness. He was feeling very dizzy and tired. He had spent the whole day with his family out there on the farm at Nkuuf and only returned in the evening. He was one of the elders who grumbled so much when they received *toi fon* from the palace messenger that night.

"His Royal Highness…" He commenced almost down his throat

"… it is just that our tradition forbids one to disrespect *toi fon*. If not, I would not have been present for this meeting because I am not really feeling fine. I have over stressed myself these last days with this planting stuff. That notwithstanding, I have this to say about the issue at hand. I condemn what the Kou people have done with all my heart. In fact, they have not acted in the brotherly love that is supposed to bind us together as offspring of the Tikak clan. This does not however mean that we should retaliate. Thank you"

With those words, he regained his seat amidst total silence and uncompromising exchange of looks among the elders that flourished for some time. Elder Kiyaan stood up to speak. He looked sharper and smarter than the first speaker. Although it was difficult to give his age, he seemed the youngest in the mists of elders who were within their late eighties and nineties.

"You have spoken well my brother. From all indication you prefer peaceful negotiation, which is good. But I am afraid if we are not careful the way we handle this issue, the people of Kou will laugh at us and look at the people of Nos as cowards. As we speak now, four sons of this land have joined our ancestors. Should we then go to them and beg for a peaceful end to a crisis whose origin we know not? We are a people with dignity. We are the biggest in land and population throughout the entire clan. We must not make ourselves a laughingstock. I therefore suggest we strike back. The youth of Nos are hungry for blood. They are out there just waiting for His Royal Highness to give them the go ahead".

Turn by turn, all the five elders present expressed their minds. From their speeches, there was no doubt that they were divided into two camps over the issue. Some were for peaceful negotiation while others were for war. Elder Kaila was the last to make a speech before His Royal Highness gave the closing remarks. Unlike others, he did not take sides:

"If we do not strike back, people will laugh at us and call us cowards. In fact, Nos would be vulnerable to attacks from neighbouring clans. If we strike, further bloodshed would be invited into this land and innocent people shall go down for it. There is an old adage that "when elephants fight it is the grass that suffers". We have to weigh the positive and negative consequences of the two sides of the coin before going in for one"

By the time the last speaker regained his seat, it was already evident that His Royal Highness was plunged into total confusion. He shook his head severally trying to come out with a solution; what now looked like a real test of his ability to take responsibilities as the leader of his people. For the first time since he took over the throne, he was face-to-face with a challenging task that needed him to employ all his wisdom to go through. What was he to do? Sacrifice the pride and dignity of his people to prevent bloodshed or declare war and plunge the fondom into chaos and anarchy? In summoning the elders, he had not foreseen this! In fact, he had not thought of the possibility of two camps emerging. In his plain and naïve mind His Royal Highness was confident that the meeting was going to be a mere formality to map out strategies on how to solve the Kou equation. And now, he had to take a decision that would increase or decrease his popularity! The Nos people were known for their bravery in the face of adversity and for their never surrendering spirit. They were always ready to fight till the last drop of their blood each time their pride was at stake. His Royal Highness knew this quite well.

The Fon of Nos recalled with nostalgic feelings how during colonisation, Nos put up one of the stiffest resistance towards the Germans. The war was the bloodiest and the colonisers were almost forced to submission. The Nos people fought with spears and locally made guns against the Germans who came with rifles and all kinds of war equipment. It was thanks to support rendered the Germans by neighbouring tribes that the Nos resistance was crushed. The people of Nos were not ready to bow down, even when it was evident that they had been defeated. The Fon of Membia was the one who took the initiative to bring peace between Nos and Germany. He took a white fowl and tied it to a long bamboo and lifted it up to indicate that Nos had surrendered, if not, the killing and bloodshed would have continued. When the Germans saw the sign, they did not understand. They misconstrued it and took it for provocation and further invitation that war should roll on. It was an elderly person from one of the tribes that had supported the Germans against Nos who made them understand that that was an indication of giving up. Since that historic war, Nos had always been feared by her neighbours and no tribe dared challenge her to a tribal war. Although the offspring of the land no longer possessed that ancestral vengeful spirit that Nos had long been known for, neighbours were still very cautious because the past had left indelible scars in their memory. It was not that Nos always emerged victorious in every battle they fought; but her Spartan and unforgiving spirit scared people away. It did not matter the seriousness of the problem for Nos to sow seeds of discord with a neighbour. They needed just something to hang on as long as the opponent would not surrender.

His Royal Highness was there in those days and had a feel of what metal the Nos people were made of. They had a unanimous instinctive belief in fighting whoever challenged them. Even most of the elders present in the palace at that moment had lived those nostalgic days. But now, he was faced with a generation of mixed ideology. Some of the youth had their fathers' blood while others were new breed that believed more on negotiation and peaceful co-existence. How was His Royal Highness going to strike a balance? How was he going to convince those who were already bracing up to attack Kou?

"My hands are tied..." His Royal Highness began in a voice that suggested the desperation within him. He had lost the steam and vigour he had before summoning the elders.

"Yet something must be done and as fast as possible. It is true that bloodshed is not good but we cannot continue to watch our people suffer humiliation in the hands of Kou. Now I suggest we go by voting. Those who think we should strike back should put up their hands." His Royal Highness waited for seconds but no hand was up. Was it that they did not get him well? For the benefit of doubt, he repeated the question and still nobody raised a hand. Was it an indication that there should be no war? His Royal Highness wondered. In order to be double sure, he asked the question the other way round, waited for seconds and still nobody put up the hand to indicate that they should go in for a peaceful negotiation. He became more confused and worried. He looked left and right expecting that someone would say something to end the sudden silence. For close to five minutes, no word was uttered. Seeing no progress, His Royal Highness got up and retired to his inner chamber without a word.

CHAPTER THREE

In the early hours of the morning that followed the meeting at the Fon's palace, the inhabitants of Nos were awoken by unusual chants and screams of children and women. Youths of the land with stern looks charged up and down the streets with spears. Some fired locally fabricated guns into the air singing war-like songs and making terrifying signals. Before it was completely dawn, they had invaded a good number of houses suspected to be those of people from Kou. Some of the inhabitants were dragged out of their houses and massacred on the streets while others were simply chased out of Nos and their properties reduced to ashes. By the time the raid was over, the damage was unspeakable. The major streets of the fondom were stained with blood and littered with tens of corpses.

Sunrise met the blood hungry youths of Nos on the way to the boundary that separated their land from that of their enemy. In every inhabited area they passed, people jumped out of bed and peeped from the window to see what was actually happening. Even those who were already up and were involved in early morning activities abandoned them and rushed back into their houses. The valiant stood on verandas with questioning looks, awed by the impending apocalypse. The war-set youths from Nos sang at the top of their voices until they faded out gradually as they disappeared from sight. Eventually, their voices could no longer be heard. However, at every point in time, a group of three or so youths, charged past to join their mates who had long gone ahead to the battle front. These were mostly those who had learned of the war much later or those who had been persuaded at the last minute to fight.

Meanwhile at the boundary, fierce fighting went on between the Nos warriors and those of Kou. There was horrific killing on both sides. Those who incurred fatal wounds were immediately carried away from the scene while those that had mild ones continued fighting and bleeding. By evening of the first day, an estimated number of fifty able bodied youths from Membia trekked to the scene of confrontation and joined the Kou warriors against Nos. this completely changed the physiognomy of the war. The intensity stepped up as Nos people too pumped in more youths. Even those who were unwilling were forced to abandon their homes to the war front. For virtually three days, the three tribes vibrated to the rhythm of a war that left behind both human and material damage.

The news that Tikak clan was falling apart spread like wildfire and media coverage soon took hold of the situation. Cameramen, radio reporters and press men from different media houses invaded the scene and were busy gathering information that was instantly disseminated within and without the country. By evening of the third day, the government dispatched ten trucks of soldiers to the clan from the nation's capital for special intervention. They were instructed to track down whoever was found with a war weapon and deal with them accordingly. The army was made up essentially of young guys just fresh from school. They were on their very first major assignment and so wanted to do everything possible to impress their boss, the minister of defence and also to make a name. News of their imminent arrival reached Tikak clan before they could even kick off and the warring youths did not wait for that to happen. The majority fled into bushes for their dear life. When the army arrived in Tikak, they acted completely against the instructions, as any youth, with or without war equipment, was arrested and seriously tortured. Some of the Tikak youths were even killed in the process while many of them sustained injuries. Peace was gradually restored in the land. Although the war came to an end, it was not without an indelible mark. Mass graves were dug and the dead buried. Those who were wounded were transported to local hospitals and health centres of Nos, Membia and Kou.

The inter-tribal war caused by the mysterious death of Wiymanla's father followed the birth of a girl child into the family. The story went that Papa Wiranyen, as the old man was fondly called, left Nos Baptist Hospital in anger immediately his son's wife was delivered of yet another girl child. The woman started labouring in a local maternity in Kou and on the third day she was transferred to Nos Baptist Hospital. Since it was rainy season and the state of the Kou earth road was not the best, a four-wheel drive vehicle was hired for 10.000 FRS CFA to carry her and a few members of the family to Nos. They left Kou at about 6pm and by few minutes to 8pm, they arrived Nos Baptist Hospital. They were welcome at the entrance, and the patient instantly transported to the emergency ward for first medical care. The rest of the delegation was asked to wait on a bench just directly opposite the emergency ward. For more than thirty minutes, there was no exchange of words between them. Wiymanla's mother bent down her head in-between her thighs and kept herself busy with Rosary prayers. She counted and recounted the beads on the string from the beginning to the end. Wiymanla walked continuously from one end of the veranda to the other constantly peeping to see if someone would come out to tell them that it was alright with his wife. At the left extreme corner of the wooden bench, Papa Wirayen sat whistling gently. He criss-crossed his legs and allowed his head to hang lazily over his hand-supported knees. Minutes after, he loosened himself from the set position and withdrew a black box of snuff from the left pocket of his jumper. He tapped the cover three times and then opened the rubber box. He dipped the tip of his right thumb right into the box and emerged with a reasonable quantity of the content. Having blocked the left nostril with the other thumb, Papa Wirayen placed the content against the right nostril and inhaled for about five seconds. He then switched to the other nostril. When he had finished with the ritual, he supported his forehead and shook his head violently. He looked visibly less worried than the other two.

At around 10pm, a nurse came out from the emergency ward full of smiles. Wiymanla and his mother rushed towards her but Papa Wirayen remained seated. He was not even looking at the direction of the nurse. Without waiting to be asked, the nurse announced:

"Congratulations sir. Your wife has been delivered of a bouncing baby girl". Upon hearing this, Papa Wirayen got up from his seat briskly and walking towards the nurse said:

"Madam, tell me it is a joke…." The nurse did not even allow him to finish.

"Papa, it is not. It is just that the child cannot be seen for now, I would have invited you people to come and confirm it yourself…"

"Hold it there woman…" Papa Wirayen thundered. "Bouncing baby what? Do female babies bounce? Then there was complete silence for some seconds, all eyes on him. He lifted his head up as he kneeled down. In a very solemn tone that could force tears out even from the eyes of a military man, he said:

"God why? Why? What have I done to deserve this? Why have you chosen to humiliate me before my age mates? Why have you cursed this family with another daughter of Eve? When will I ever hear the cry of a male grandchild before I join my ancestors? When will I also head a delegation to another compound to pay for my grand child's bride price?" Then, in a split second, he got on his feet started cursing in every direction as he walked away. Wirayen's mother tried to calm him down but to no avail. It even looked like the more they tried, the more he was worked up. This did not however prevent the woman from continuing:

"Papa Wirayen, you are taking the issue too far. Children are a gift from God and we must accept them with joy no matter the sex. Remember you have high blood pres…"

"Oh woman, don't give me that sermon. When a full-blooded man gives birth to five girls in a roll, we cannot continue to deceive ourselves that these are gifts from God". He cut in and without waiting for further exchange turned and was gone.

The three others stood there with their mouths ajar wandering. The nurse shook her head and left. Wiymanla exchanged looks with his mother but none of them had something to say. He bent down his head and was soon plunged into unending thoughts. He remembered that after the birth of the fourth consecutive girl child into his family, his father had told him that he would not forgive him should his wife give birth to another girl child. Papa Wirayen had even threatened to commit suicide and hang his blood on Wiymanla's head should that happen. How was he to control that? After the third girl child, Wiymanla and his wife had sought for advice from a medical doctor who gave them directives on when to conceive if they were looking for a male child. They followed this to the end but it did not work. They had planned to have four children and were forced to go in for the fifth because of pressure from the family, especially Papa Wirayen who wanted a male child at all cost. The pregnancy for the fifth child was delayed for almost two years because they wanted to do everything possible to conceive a male child. They went to medical and native doctors as well as men of God of all kinds and were assured that everything would be alright. When his wife took in, every necessary ecography was done and there were signs that it was a male child. He could not understand why it had turned out to be the contrary. Was it a punishment from God for wanting to change His will in his life?

But why was he killing himself? Wiymanla wondered! Were there not people in other homes dying to have just a child, no matter the sex? If God has decided to bless him only with female children why should he want to change His will?

Besides, his female children were a source of pride to him. They were doing exceptionally well in school. Why then should he ask too much from God? Instantly, Wiymanla resolved that his wife would not conceive again. Enough was enough and if his father wanted to curse him because he could not give him a male child, so be it. After all he had tried more than his father who was able to father only him and his younger sister.

CHAPTER FOUR

When Papa Wirayen briskly walked away that night from the hospital, nobody took the old man seriously. Wiymanla and his mother waved it aside as one of the empty threats he had been noted for. He had done that on several occasions and ended up coming back to his decision. Mama Wirayen could still vividly recall that some years ago her husband asked her to leave his house because he saw her with the parish priest one Sunday night. They were standing at the entrance to the parish in the late hours of the evening, discussing and laughing like young lovers still burning with youthful exuberance. That was not the first time she had a misunderstanding with her husband over the issue of the priest. They used to quarrel and at times fight whenever Papa Wirayen learned that his wife prepared food and took to the parish. He was always angry that she selected the best parts of chicken, fish or meat and reserved them for *Father* while he, the man of the house and the bread winner of the family had to contend himself with second grade pieces.

Whenever there was not enough food, Mama Wirayen preferred to starve the entire household, but not *Father*! She insisted that as the president of the Catholic Women's Association (CWA), it was her prerogative to make sure that *Father* was well fed. This soon brought a rift between her and other CWA members who were not happy at all. They accused her of violating the constitution of the Association which gave the right to every CWA member to prepare food for *Father* only once in a month. But they were afraid of confronting her. Nobody had the guts to dare the Iron Mama, as she was fondly called in the village! The women bore the grudge silently and gossiped only among themselves. Iron Mama eventually eavesdropped one of such gossips and instantly summoned an extra-ordinary general meeting of CWA. She wanted to make certain things clear to the members.

As soon as those who showed up for the meeting were seated, Iron Mama took the floor from her sitting position without any formality.

"In my capacity as the incumbent president of Kou CWA, I have summoned this meeting to make a few things straight to those of you overrunning your mouths on things you know nothing about. I want to warn you to leave me out of your gossips. How I lead my life is none of your business. Is it my fault that I am the most beautiful lady in this village? Is it?"

Mama Kingum who had been boiling with anger and tapping her left foot on the ground throughout did not allow her to continue. She jumped up from her seat unceremoniously, arranged the CWA loin on her waist, adjusted her blouse and started untying her head scarf saying:

"Jezebel, you have overstepped the boundary and if you are not careful you will soon stumble. You think people are quite because they do not know about your secret dealings in this village? Public toilet... *hururururuuuuh Kwarah*. Look, let me tell you, you are a disgrace to womanhood. You are..."

Iron Mama did not allow her to take it to the end. In one skip like a kangaroo after a prey, she leaped for Mama Kingum

26

who, sensing danger, had also skipped to confront her. The two met midway in the air and went crashing onto the bare hard earth like *Kontry cocks* that had run out of patience with each other. Iron Mama was a very fat woman with hipped buttocks that protruded behind her like cargo on the back of someone on transhumance. She was soon seen exerting her heavy weight on Mama Kingum. Mama Kingum, with her smallish size struggled in vain to push her away. They both ripped each other apart with their overgrown fingernails. Cross-lines as those left on the ground by a dog in display with its claws could be seen drizzling with blood from their faces. They rolled from one end of the meeting ground to the other, hitting each other and cursing. Mama Kingum too was not an easy walk-over. She gave her opponent tough times tearing every piece of cloth on her. She tore off Iron Mama's blouse and divided her brassieres into two. When Iron Mama noticed the damage, she opened her mouth as wide as that of a crocodile and sank her teeth into Mama Kingum's jaw. Blood oozed out staining all of them in the process. The other women who had been struggling all this while to separate the fight realised that there was nothing they could do to lift Iron Mama who was literarily squeezing her opponent. They started hitting her with any object they could find around as Mama Kingum screamed for help. This did not yield any fruit. It was thanks to the timely arrival of three or so men that the two women could be disentangled. Virtually naked, the two women who were were guarded to their various houses.

News of the incident made headlines in Kou and beyond. The CWA members of the parish became a subject of mockery in the entire village. People said all sorts of things about them.

But the general feeling was that they had failed in their duty. They had disgraced Holy Mary, the mother of Jesus, whose exemplary lifestyle they were supposed to emulate. The women themselves felt very bad and admitted that what had happened did not reflect an Association of that calibre. In order to save face, the few of them who still had CWA at heart met and designated a delegation to the parish priest. They wanted him to suggest what should be done, especially the two members who had dragged the Association's name through the mire. *Father* told them that it was not his position to take a decision on the issue. He had to write first to the Diocesan Bishop and he would instruct him on what to do. The CWA were asked to wait until he received the opinion of hierarchy. Two weeks came and passed yet no reaction from the parish priest. A delegation again went there and he told them that the Bishop was still to react. They were once more urged to be patient. This went on for two months.

On Assumption Day, the CWA decided to take law into their hands. They took *Father* by surprise. He had just given the last blessings and concluded mass with the mechanical sentence, "go in peace the mass is ended", when he saw a queue of roughly forty-three women in CWA uniform moving towards the altar in a solemn manner. They came, bowed and took position just at the front of the altar. The leader of the congregation started talking almost immediately.

"Kou faithful congregation. I greet you all. What we are about to do now should not be a surprise to anyone. You should instead be surprised that we took such a long time to do it. It was due to reasons beyond our control. I know you have a lot to do so we shall not take much of your time. Meeting at an extra-ordinary meeting yesterday, the CWA decided as follows". She paused to bring out a sheet of paper that was folded and inserted in her loin just slightly below her waist. She unrolled the sheet and then continued:

" as I was saying, we met in an extra-ordinary meeting and decided as follows

1)   For initiating a fight thereby acting contrary to the rules governing the Association meant to emulate the lifestyle of our mother The Blessed Virgin Mary, Mama Wirayen has been relieved of her duty as the president of CWA;

2)   Henceforth, she is a non member of CWA for an undetermined period;

3)   On her part, Mama Kingum is suspended for twelve months for openly insulting and inciting a member of CWA to a fight;

4)   From the moment of this pronouncement, its application goes into effect, here and now.

We would like to invite the two persons concerned to move forward."

In shame, heads down, Iron Mama and Mama Kingum walked to the front and stood before the congregation. The CWA members circled the two women and started stripping them of the CWA uniform. The congregation chanted and other whistled provocatively. *Father* was tongue-tied as he watched the scene from a standing position. In a matter of minutes, the ritual was over and Iron Mama as well as Mama Kingum was given different loin cloth to put on.

Dust was still to settle fully on the incident concerning Mama Wiranyen and the CWA when she was involved in yet another scandal. Papa Wiranyen was returning from *Mfuh* late into the night when he had taken enough liquor to stupor. *Mfuh* was once in a week and meant only for men! On that particular day, every man in the Tikak clan was proud to belong to that secret society in which no woman or an underage was allowed to be part. Men danced round *Kimbankar* singing rhythmic songs that neither had clear wordings nor specific messages. *Kimbankar*, the big wooden drum, stood on three or so legs and was often placed at the centre with one man as the drummer. Each man aesthetically danced round in a circle hitting two machetes against one another. From time to time, two excited men would single out themselves, and display. Each of them thrust one machete into *Kiburuh* and lifted up the other towards the partner in total euphoria. They then clang two machetes against each other and shouted in excitement.

Mfuh was indeed an energetic dance that required a lot of display and demonstration. Whenever its members had danced for roughly thirty minutes, they thrust their machetes into *Kiburuh* and sat down to sip some palm wine before continuing. They sat round a big clay jar that stood at the centre. It was always filled to the brim with palm wine. Someone would volunteer and take up *Ngif* that floated on top of the big jar like an abandoned bundle in a sea. He filled the small calabash with palm wine and went round sharing. Only those who had *Bar* were privileged to drink as they wanted. Whoever came without one had to wait until someone had sipped at least ten cups and was satisfied. Only then could he surrender his *Bar* if he felt like doing so. But there were some men who quietly returned their traditional cups back to their bags as soon as they had sipped enough palm wine. After all, they were not obliged to share their *Bar* with someone! Whenever *Ngif* was empty, the sharer went back to the centre, refilled it with more palm wine and continued the sharing exercise. Once the spirit of the *Mfuh* was worked up and energy regained, they returned to the circle and dancing continued.

It was after such an exciting evening that Papa Wirayen, really tipsy, under the influence of alcohol, was feeling his way home. His *Kiburuh* that was held on both ends of his waist by a rope dangled on the side virtually disturbing his movement. He swung from one end of the narrow path to another, murmuring to himself like someone unstable upstairs. Each time he heard a suspicious sound or noise, Papa Wirayen adjusted the *Kiburuh* and pressed it against his armpit holding the thrust machete from the handle in readiness for self defence. He was indeed a replica of most *Mfuh* members. On that particular day, they went back home tipsy because there was always enough alcohol. It was a by-weekly routine that kept men of Kou late outside.

In his hollow state, Papa Wirayen decided to take the small path that cut through the parish cemetery to his house. There were usually strange stories about that path but that particular night, he was too tipsy to plunge himself into such fairy tales. When he had successively gone past the cemetery and was at the outlet he faintly perceived two people in what looked like white regalia. They were so close to each other in an entanglement that caught his attention, but it was extremely

31

difficult to determine who they were from that distance. Papa Wirayen stopped and wiped his eyes with the back of his palm. His blood ran chill and the drunkenness that was in his eyes cleared up instantly. He looked again but the darkness that had taken hold of the night impaired his vision. He removed his machete from the *Kiburuh* and started moving towards the figures. Suddenly someone laughed hysterically from the entanglement with a voice as sharp as that of his wife.

The laughter continued as if the person was continuously tickled by someone. Papa Wirayen called his wife's name and listened but nobody answered. All was again silent! He became very frightened and knew that it was a matter of life and death. Papa Wirayen lifted up his machete and began charging towards the figures. They broke up and started running. He removed his torch from the traditional bag that hung carelessly across his left shoulder, switched it on and pointed it directly in front of him. The rays fell on someone in white cassock and another one in a blouse that looked exactly like the one his wife wore on that day. He accelerated after them stumbling and getting up but could not catch up with them. Papa Wirayen came to a halt when he saw one side of an abandoned shoe of a woman. He picked it up and noticed that it was that of his wife. Breathing like a cat that had just survived the claws of a dog, he retired home. That night he did not sleep. His mind was haunted by all kinds of ideas.

In the early morning of the next day, Mama Wirayen came home. Her husband was standing at the veranda and she passed into the room without greeting him. He followed her in and stood looking at her as she sat on the bed. He thought of beating her up but immediately remembered that in the past, it had not been a successful attempt. He recalled with scorn that on several occasions, neighbours had had to rescue him from the hands of that *wall of a woman*! Mama Wirayen was a real thorn in his flesh and he could do nothing about it. All the while that he stood staring at her, she did not seem to neither notice him nor blink. She went about doing her things as if nobody had entered the house. In a feeble voice that quivered as if the speaker was suffering from an uncontrollable fit, Papa Wirayen told her to pack her things and leave his house immediately. He added that he did not want to see any of her belongings when he returned from the market in the evening. But when he came back in the evening, Mama Wirayen was still there. She did not bulge. Papa Wirayen simply licked his lips and remained quiet. What else could he do?

CHAPTER FIVE

And so, when Papa Wirayen left the hospital that night, everybody knew that he would come home as soon as his anger must have subsided. That was why it did not occur to Wiymanla and his mother to run after him. They waited outside the labour room for close to an hour with the hope that the hospital authorities would let them in to see the mother and the new-born. Instead, another nurse came out and announced to them that the child had been put in the incubator and was not supposed to be visited by anybody until after a couple of days. Only the mother and the doctor incharge were to have access to the child during that time. The mother was to go there on specific times, to breastfeed the baby, and the doctor was to attend to her medically. The child's mother could not also be seen that night because she had lost so much blood in the process and needed some rest and recovery. Wiymanla and his mother were given a place in the hospital to spend the night.

By the next day, Wiymanla's wife was already up on her feet even though she had not yet fully recovered. It was total joy that animated the environment when the three of them met especially as Wiymanla and his mother were reassured that the child was doing quite fine. After having spent some time together, Wiymanla decided to go back to Kou to let the people know the situation. Their departure the previous night had created a lot of suspense back home and it was necessary to clear it up. Mama Wirayen had to remain in the hospital because the mother of the child was still too weak and constantly needed assistance. Wiymanla gave them some money and left for Kou promising to be back first thing the following day. He was lucky to board the first car and by 9: 30am he was in Kou.

As was expected, Wiymanla's arrival brought a lot of relief to other family members who had been very worried throughout. He narrated the ordeal they went through to eager villagers who listened attentively with mouths ajar. When he had finished, he tried to enquire if they had seen his father. The villagers were instead taken aback. They wondered how they were to know his whereabouts when he had travelled to Nos with Wiymanla and the others the previous night. By evening, no news was heard about Papa Wirayen. What looked like a child's play began to create confusion and a dark cloud over the minds of family members. Gripped by fear, they spent every second wondering what must have happened to him. It soon became known in the entire village that Papa Wirayen was missing. A collective search was launched. The villagers visited every place where they suspected he could be.

By late into the night of the first day, the news of the disappearance of Papa Wirayen had spread like wildfire. Everybody noticed his absence from his famous *Kiban* in Kou market square where he usually sold *Shinjaan* and *Viluh*. This was very unusual. People liked to buy castor oil and honey from him because he "measured well" and sold quality products unlike others who diluted theirs with water or any other substance to have much quantity and make more profit. Besides, he was very generous and down to earth with everybody. The people of Kou could not come to terms with the sudden disappearance of this popular man whose presence at the market square had been conspicuous for over three decades. He was known by everybody in Kou. Other dealers in the same products were not happy with him and saw him as a threat. Until Papa Wirayen's *Shinjaan* and *Viluh* were finished customers did not want to buy elsewhere. Whenever he was absent, something that hardly occurred, it made headlines amongst his colleagues because they knew they would sell. They therefore received the news of his disappearance with mixed feelings!

On the second day, there was still no trace of Papa Wirayen. An open manhunt beyond the borders of Kou was launched. People went to every nook and cranny in and out of the village. His Royal Highness dispatched a delegation to Membia to visit one of the most powerful witch doctors in the clan. Wiymanla headed the delegation that embarked on the odious journey to Membia. Wherever a vehicle was available, they took it and where it stopped they continued on foot. Each time they met someone along the way who could provide them with any information, they did not hesitate to approach the person. But by the time the delegation reached Membia, they had had no reliable information from anybody on the way. They went straight to *Ntoh* Membia. His Royal Highness was not in. He had gone on a forty-five-kilometre journey to do some sacrifices at the boundary as he often did once in a while. His absence was not felt so much as the delegation was given a befitting welcome by *Vikiyntoh*. The number of queen mothers in *Ntoh* Membia was so alarming that if they all had to cook for the delegation, it would take one month for Wiymanla and his team to finish the food. Five young and agile queen mothers were asked by the eldest to take care of them the way Membia women do to visitors. She also instructed *Tchinda*, the Fon's messenger, to slaughter the biggest cock around. The five queen mothers tasked with cooking hurried up and in no time, *Kiban wuna nyoh seji* was ready.

They munched the huckleberry and corn fufu meal without any reservation. From the way they ate, it was evident that they were starving. But Wiymanla was completely lost in thoughts. The disappearance of his father kept on haunting his memory. He still wondered where the old man could be and whether he was still alive or dead wherever he was. He did not want to think of the second option because if it were to happen, then he was finished. What would the villagers say? How would he convince them that he knew nothing about his father's death? The way they reasoned *hmmm!* It was not going to be possible to stop them from spreading that he had sacrificed his father in *Minyongu* to have money. God forbid! He said it somewhere in his throat and bent down to eat.

When they had finished eating, Tchinda supplied them with enough palm wine to wash down the food. It was now time to get into the crux of the matter. Wiymanla explained what had brought them on such a long journey. Everybody was taken by surprise! The people of Membia had neither heard of the birth of the new-born nor the disappearance of Papa Wirayen. Everybody wondered where the old man could have gone to. They concluded that he could certainly not be in Membia, otherwise somebody would have seen him and rushed him to the palace. Even if he were dead, his corpse would have been discovered especially by one of those hunters who toured almost the entire fondom, day and night, in search of animals. The way these hunters went about their activities showed that the campaign against indiscriminate killing of certain species of wild animals did not mean anything to them.

After minutes of silent meditation, all eyes and ears were turned towards Ba Ngwang to come up with an idea. He was the only person in the land whose services His Royal Highness often sought whenever the land was confronted with a problem that beat his intelligence. Ba Ngwang had been nicknamed *Sifon* because people claimed he was so full of common sense and wisdom that he could only be equated to the Fon's eye. And truly, Ba Ngwang had lived up to the challenge. So many years ago, Membia and Banfoum had a long clash that stemmed from power struggle between rulers of the two fondoms. That clash had left a scar whose magnitude was measured in the tensed relationship between the two tribes.

The clash originated from a misunderstanding between *Vikiyntoh* of the two fondoms. Membia *Vikiyntoh* had gone to till a piece of land at the boundary in preparation for the rainy season. They realised that Banfoum *Vikiyntoh* had been there the previous day and had failed to respect the demarcation by stretching some fifty centimetres into their side. The Membia queen mothers decided to direct an erosion channel into the farms of their counterparts from *Ntoh* Banfoum. That night, there was heavy rainfall. The running water penetrated into Banfoum side and washed away all the newly tilled ridges that their women had made. In the early hours of the next day after the second cock crow Membia fondom was invaded by unidentified men from Banfoum. Their target was the palace and before the inhabitants could comprehend what was happening, they had made away with His Royal Highness and the eldest *Wirntoh*. The two had been taken captive and carried to Banfoum palace. Membia men tried to enter Banfoum to recover their ruler but there was no way. Banfoum was well prepared and from all indications, they had taken quite some time and put in place a good network before invading Membia. Some of the Membia men were captured, severely tortured and chased out of the Banfoum. The entire Membia land mobilised and launched another unsuccessful attempt to enter Banfoum. Banfoum men were stationed at every entrance to the land fully armed.

The Fon of Membia and the queen mother were locked up in a room in Banfoum palace. The Membia people waited impatiently for the release of their ruler. Days turned into weeks, yet Banfoum was not ready to let go the royal family. The way things unfolded, was such that the people of Membia would go on for long without anybody occupying the royal throne. Something had to be done to salvage the situation! Ba Ngwang brought together few elders for them to concert and come up with a solution. They came to a unanimous decision that somebody had to occupy the throne for the time being. The next worry was to choose the right person who was fit to wear such heavy and big shoes. Everything taken into consideration, Shufai Koko was the only man in the land on whose head such a daunting task could be placed. Upon concertation, his candidature was rejected by the majority. The argument advanced was that he was an opportunist who, if given the chance to occupy the royal throne, would never leave it again for whatever reason. Even if the present Fon, now in captivity, were to return to the land, sometime to come, it would take a bloody clash for Shufai Koko to be removed from that throne. Besides, people hated him because he was too much of a conservative. He was one of those few who would hang on to every traditional value as long as possible and would not care about its effect on the people. He had stood against attempts by the elites from Membia to put an end to female genital mutilation. He equally refused the termination of breast ironing practised on young girls. The argument that such practices were dangerous to human health did not augur well to him who stood his grounds and maintained that those who said breast ironing could lead to breast cancer were cowards and killers of tradition! In his opinion, those practices were handed down to them by their ancestors and they had to be preserved jealously.

It was therefore decided that Shufai Koko could not fit squarely into those shoes. Ba Ngwang then suggested that Shufai Kindze be given such responsibilities because, to him, that was the only person qualified to sit on the throne temporarily. The elders looked critically into the proposal and saw that Ba Ngwang was right! Truly, Shufai Kindze could confidently steer the ship along. He was a good organiser and Membia people respected him a lot because of his humility and achievements. He had offered the youngest queen mother to the palace. The leopard skin on which His Royal Highness usually placed his feet was brought to the palace by him after he hunted down a leopard alone. Then, during the German versus Nos war, it was Shufai Kindze who provided a white fowl that was used to bring about a peaceful end to the clash. The achievements were so enormous that His Royal Highness decided to elevate him from a mere "Fai" to a "Shufai". That meant he had been lifted to a position that gave him the right to fit in virtually all the traditional circles with others and decide on issues that concerned the land. This brought serious conflict between him and other traditional rulers. Shufai Nkem was particularly bitter about the decision. He said Shufai Kindze did not deserve it because anybody could still achieve what he had achieved. To him, His Royal Highness did that out of selfish interest. He said the title was a kind of appreciation for the young wife Shufai Kindze had given the palace. His Royal Highness wanted to deceive his in-law with the title to lobby for more. Shufai Nkem bragged round that if His Royal Highness wanted beautiful young girls, he could provide them. The question on every lip was "how could someone who had five boys and without a grandson be able to provide young beautiful queens for the Fon?"

It was not easy to convince Shufai Kindze to accept the throne. He refused categorically that it was against the tradition to want him to be the acting Fon when the real person was still alive. "What would happen when he eventually comes back?" He questioned. The council of elders admitted that his worry was quite pertinent, yet they insisted that the throne could not be left empty. Somebody needed to occupy and move on with traditional rites for the time being, if not, the ancestors of the land would not be happy. Besides, tradition demanded that for someone to carry that out, he ought to be vested with royal powers. That was only possible when the person was seated on the throne and certain rituals performed on him. After the rituals, the person was fortified to communicate with the gods and ancestors of the land. Even after all these explanations,

Shufai Kindze was still very reluctant to take up the challenge. He stood his grounds with the view that Membia people were concerned with short term measures and did not consider its long-term effects on the land! Shufai Kindze realised that despite his resistance, the council of elders was not ready to bow. The issue was beginning to create a rift between him and his people, something he never wished for! How could he alone continue to stand against the decision of the entire land? Even his family members were urging him to let go! And so, seeing that the pressure was more than he could bear, he eventually gave in spite of himself!

For months, the people of Banfoum were not willing to free the ruler of Membia. The room where the royal family was kept was heavily guarded, day and night. One day, something mysterious happened that left Banfoum in bewilderment. The Fon of Banfoum had asked the guards to bring the Fon of Membia before him for questioning on a number of issues. When they opened the door there was nobody inside. They searched around and to their greatest dismay they saw him walking away with the queen mother. The Fon of Banfoum ordered that he be captured and brought back. The guards charged after him but he kept strolling and going. They soon realised that the closer they moved the more an invisible force pulled them away from the royal family. Then what happened next, they could not believe their eyes. The royal family soon leapt into the air and suddenly transformed into two hawks and were flying away majestically and provocatively. Everybody stood watching at the mysterious sight benumbed. They had heard about mysterious happenings, they had dreamed about supernatural occurrences, but never had they ever lived it live the way they were living it now! His Royal Highness, the Fon of Banfoum could not believe his eyes. With his hand supporting his chin, he shook his head violently and shouted "No, Noooh, this cannot be happening". They watched until the two hawks disappeared from sight. Their eyes continued staring the sky as if they were expecting the sight to be rewound and rolled on again in a slow motion for a better viewing.

The royal family arrived Membia late that evening amidst a standing ovation that lasted for virtually thirty minutes. When the Membia people first saw the two hawks flying towards the palace, nobody knew what they were. But the sizes of the hawks gave everybody a feeling of a strange sight; even village hunters were amazed. Never had they ever seen a hawk of that gigantic size. They watched, waiting for them to land. The two hawks circled in the sky for a very long time as people gathered anxiously waiting to see what would happen next. When the open courtyard was already full to capacity, the hawks gradually came down. By the time they touched the ground, there was a sudden sharp flash that almost blinded everybody. In a split second, the Membia people saw the royal family standing in front of them. People ululated, chanted praises and sang victory songs in honour of the royal couple. His Royal Highness ordered the land to be thrown in a festive mood for three good days!

Late that night, Shufai Kindze and his family left Membia for no specific destination. Although nobody asked him to go away, he felt that that was the best thing to do. How was the land going to accommodate two Fons? Even if he had sat there temporarily, he had somehow been ruling and the people had been giving him the royalties due a Fon. How then was it suddenly going to happen that those royalties would cease? It was not going to be easy for him and the returned Fon to cohabit. He felt that somehow, there was going to be an uncomfortable air blowing between them. Another possible solution was to declare Kindze compound another fondom. Again that was a new way of sowing seeds of everlasting discord between people with a common ancestry. Where were the people of Membia going to pay allegiance if Kindze compound was made a fondom? These thoughts had run through his mind and he came to the conclusion that the best solution was to leave the land with his family and settle somewhere far away from Membia. They trekked throughout the night and by morning of the following day, they arrived Nos. They went straight to the palace and Shufai Kindze explained the situation to the Fon of Nos. He offered to settle him and his family in his land until things were sorted out.

The people of Membia were surprised when they got to the palace for the three-day celebration to continue and noticed the conspicuous absence of Shufai Kindze and the family. Upon investigation it was realised that Shufai Kindze had deserted the land with his family. His Royal Highness was taken aback! He did not understand why the man that was venerated in the entire fondom by all could take such an impulsive decision without even informing anybody. Personally, as a man who understood tradition, the Fon knew that Shufai Kindze was right to reason out the way he did, but His Royal Highness refused to accept that walking away was the best option. He argued that he ought to have allowed the council of elders to take a decision. How were they ever to make the outside world understand that Shufai Kindze and the family were not exiled from the land because he illegally occupied the throne when the man in charge was still alive? In the face of such controversy, it was Ba Ngwang who advised the Fon on what decision to take. He suggested that he should be allowed to head a delegation of elders to where Shufai Kindze and the family were perching. Their mission was to use every peaceful means possible to bring him back to the land.

Convincing Shufai Kindze to return to Membia was again another tough venture. It was more of a herculean   task than Ba Ngwang had expected. The first time they went there, Shufai Kindze refused to talk to them. He sat in a thinking position throughout their visit with his two hands against his jaws, eyes fixed on the ground before him. Ba Ngwang urged him to say something, apologising on behalf of the entire land for what they had pushed him into, but he remained still and motionless like someone in a trance. What he was thinking of, no man could tell. May be he was thinking about how the people would welcome him back to the land, perhaps he was worried about what the relationship with His Royal Highness would now be or he pondered on whether to sacrifice his integrity that was at stake for the land or not! Nobody could tell because there was no trace on his indifferent face to betray what unfolded in his psyche. The delegation sat there stuck and bemoaned, not knowing what to do next! They had been sitting there for the past three hours and that did not seem to bother Shufai Kindze. He was constant and unshakable in his game of motionless gazing and could go on and on for an undetermined number of hours. Ba Ngwang asked the delegation to start off for Membia. He might have been successful in the past in the face of situations like this but that was not going to be in this case, at least, not for that day! Ba Ngwang felt that a different strategy was to be adopted for another day to bring a son of the soil back to the land!

Following feedback from the adventure to Shufai Kindze, there was a heated debate in the council of elders. One fraction, headed by Shufai Koko, held that Shufai Kindze and the family should be slammed a sanction of definite exile for spitting on the face of Membia fondom. He, in particular, maintained that his colleague had committed sacrilege and therefore had to endure the consequences. That was contrary to Ba Ngwang's opinion. He was one of the few people who argued that the council of elders should still delegate some people to go and plead with Shufai Kindze. He pressed on saying:

"If we do not go again, it will be like we just went to tease him when we did not mean it. It will be like we went to mock him when in reality we did not want him back in the land. Let's try the second time and when he turns it down, we would have a justifiable reason before the ancestors"

By the time Shufai Koko and his camp noticed that Ba Ngwang opinion's was beginning to hold water, they staged a walk out from the meeting ground saying that they could not be party to irrational decisions. A week later, a bigger delegation, with *Nwerong* at its head, poured into the compound where Shufai Kindze and the family were perching. When Shufai Kindze saw this, his blood ran chill. He did not want to believe his eyes. Had it come to that? He asked himself. Who was he to defile *Nwerong*, the most powerful juju in the land? He immediately took the floor without waiting for the purpose of the mission to be unveiled:

"*Nwerong* Membia, My people, I did not refuse your call in the past because I despised you or my land. *Nyaaamoo. Boh dze kikoy*, may the ancestors forbid that! Who am I to turn my back to the land? Who am I to bite the finger that fed me? When a bird flies and flies far up into the air, it must perch somewhere. And no matter the number of times it perches, it must return to its abode. Membia is my abode and I have to retire there because there is no place like home. It was just that I needed some time to put myself together. Now I have done that and I am ready to go with you people."

CHAPTER SIX

Ba Ngwang was the most experienced among those in the palace during the impromptu visit of the delegation from Kou. He was expected to do something and he himself felt the pressure. In a thinking position, Ba Ngwang supported his jaws with both hands and thought for some time. Then, one hand left the right jaw to his beardless chin and he caressed it aimlessly. At some point, he ran his fingers through his baldhead and hit it gently as if asking for wisdom that could only be found on that head that had experienced decades of baldness. After close to a minute of thinking, he gave a wry smile and said:

"Yes...the solution lies in visiting a native doctor. There is one in this land that would not disappoint us. He has proven his worth in circumstances like this, countless number of times"

The idea was welcomed by everybody. Even if Wiymanla was not very much comfortable with it, he had no choice at that moment. He was very desperate to find out the whereabouts of his father and would do anything to arrive at that. He licked his lips and said

"Then what are we still waiting for? Let's go straight away!

Two other guys and Ba Ngwang joined the delegation from Kou for the fact-finding mission that was to last for barely an hour. It was about 3pm that they left for the native doctor's village some four kilometres away from the palace. Ba Ngwang was in his early eighties and in the group. Although he still looked very strong and tried as much as possible to give the impression that he could still undertake such journeys for a decade or so, age line had really crept in and rendered him less active. He could no longer walk as fast as he used to. But that afternoon he kept the front line as if in competition with the rest of the crew members. He shared his experiences with the rest and cracked jokes that kept them going tirelessly. When they had gone for a kilometre or two, he temporarily brought the voyage to a halt to explain to them that at that point, they had to abandon the main road and undertake an odious journey on a path that meandered through a thick forest down to a sombre and frightful valley. He also cautioned them to watch out because the path was a basking site for reptiles like tortoises, lizards and snakes especially in a hot afternoon like that one! Everybody developed goose bumps, and one by one, they took some steps behind. Without waiting for any question or further reactions, Ba Ngwang removed his machete from his *Kiburuh* and led the way through the overgrown path that made movement quite difficult. They quietly walked through the narrow path amidst elephant grass stems that criss-crossed in a disorderly manner. With his machete up and ready to bring down anything that posed a problem, Ba Ngwang tore apart grass to make a penetrable passage where he judged there was practically none! Then, all of a sudden, a cobra emerged from its basking abode and was moving towards them. Midway, it stopped, reared up and spread its skin behind the head, forming a hood. It suspended its head in the air, staring at them steadily without blinking. Its venomous tongue kept on going in and coming out, quivering from one side of the mouth to the other. Ba Ngwang asked everybody to stop and stand on one side behind him. Once that was done, he stepped forward and addressed the cobra:

"We are friends and not enemies, messenger of the gods. This machete you see is simply for self defence and nothing else! We have come because the land is on fire and only Docta can quench it. Please make way for us…"

As soon as he had finished talking, the cobra coiled back gently and brought down its head. Few seconds later, it turned and shuffled away, meandering through the grass until it could be seen no more. The others stood for a while lost in amazement! They could not believe their eyes as they gazed round and quivered in fright at any noise heard or imagined. For the time being, none of them was willing to take a step further or backward! Ba Ngwang stood transfixed for basically half a minute shaking his head. With a wry smile, he scrutinised round for some time and then motioned for the rest to follow him. They came pouring after him almost on their toes like children seeking for safety following a thunder strike. Wiymanla made sure that he was close to Ba Ngwang as much as possible with the hope that he would shield him in case of another danger. Like a hollow man in the face of adversity, he hung on Ba Ngwang who had become his support staff. The hissing of snakes, the persistent mewing of unseen cats and the constant cry of an owl made the surrounding quite scaring and uncomfortable. After a short walk from the site where they encountered the cobra, the delegation perceived the native doctor's shrine not at a distance. Everybody heaved a sigh of relief except for

Wiymanla who kept on panting like a hunting dog. He wanted to abandon the journey halfway and go back home. Yet, the very thought of the cobra they met on the way made him to shrink. How was he to walk past that very spot alone in the midst of those horrible sounds ensuing from every corner of the forest? He thought and immediately dismissed the idea of going back. He was convinced that moving ahead with the others was the better of the two evils because with them, he was sure to receive maximum support in case of any danger.

As they approached the shrine, his fear was gradually transformed into admiration of the fine art that issued from the place. It was rare of its kind and offered him spectacle that was to remain in his memory for a very long time. Two long coiled horns of probably a deer projected themselves from a skull slightly hung above the threshold of the door that was held together by frames aesthetically decorated with rare sculpture. Wiymanla was marvelled. He examined it closely trying to decipher the different reptiles that were carved on the wood. He could discern faintly that the dominant reptile captured in that sculpture was a lizard. Even if he was unable to tell what other creatures were designed on that exquisitely elaborate art, he enjoyed every bit of it all the same. He hastily concluded that it had been done by either a specialist from Kou or someone closer to that ethnic group. In the entire region and even beyond, the Kou people were noted for their gift in sculpture. Each time there was an art exhibition anywhere in the country and a sculptor was invited from Kou, the spectacle was always an indelible one. Foreigners travelled from other countries right to this little-known ethnic group to buy their end product!

Mbashi, aka Docta, as people fondly called him, was present when Ba Ngwang and the others reached the shrine. He was busy boiling herbs of all sorts and putting them into containers. Ba Ngwang knocked and entered with the others except Wiymanla who was still struggling to remove his shoes and had not noticed that others had gone in without doing so. He was probably reasoning instinctively that Docta was not like most native doctors who would oblige people to take off their shoes before entering their shrine. Docta asked him not to bother himself and reminded him that in his shrine there was no formality just for the sake of it. They all sat facing Docta. Meanwhile, Wiymanla did not take off his eyes from the walls that fed his inquisitive mind with much to take home. The type of things that were on those walls and on a stick pinned at the centre of the floor made his heart to palpitate for some seconds before regaining its normal beat. Small traditional bags, made of *Susu* produced from palm fronds were almost everywhere. In black and brown colours, they imposed themselves visibly bulging with their contents meant for the treatment from different illnesses. The bags were so many that Wiymanla wondered how this middle-aged man was able to distinguish each of the contents from the other! The resemblance between the bags, their congested appearance and the apparent carelessness with which they were displayed all made him to believe that the man used something beyond natural powers to avoid mix-up. But then, he thought again, if a pharmacist could serve people without being confused, with all types of drugs at his disposal, why should Docta not do it too?

Wiymanla continued feeding his seemingly tireless eyes. He rolled them round the place and eventually rested them on a heavily decorated kitchen-chair almost as black as charcoal. That was another site of wonder! He did not want to continue looking at it for fear that Docta may think that he, Wiymanla, had come all the way to study his shrine. Wiymanla immediately took his eyes off the far end of the floor and held them down right in front of him. He did not notice when he had lifted them back to the walls again. A large frame that bore the full names and picture of Docta was displayed closer to where Wiymanla sat. As he paid more attention to the content of the frame, he realised that it was a legal document signed by the Minister of Culture recognising Docta as a tradi-practitioner. Once more, he brought down his head determined not to lift it up for further scrutiny lest he create a false impression about himself.

Docta collected *Bing* from the stick at the centre of the floor. He held it with his left hand and used his right hand to rotate the stick protruding from the mouth of the small calabash. He was some sort of stirring it so that the content should be well mixed. When he was convinced that the mixture was alright, he withdrew the small stick. Some black liquid was stuck round the stick. He placed it against his left thumb and dragged it on different spots seven times. Each time he did the dragging, some quantity of the liquid was deposited on the spot. He turned his thumb upside down and licked it admirably. Then from one person to the other, he deposited the liquid in the similar manner and urged them to lick as he himself had done. Others had little or no difficulty in doing so. Wiymanla did not like the colour of the liquid. When Docta deposited it on his thumb he observed it closely, contemplating on whether to lick or throw it away. He looked at the others from face to face and noticed that they were all fine. Nobody showed signs of negative effect of the liquid in him. He covered his eyes and tasted it first. It was good, very good that he found himself licking his thumb constantly in a stupefying manner. He wanted to clamour for more but the very thought that it was the first time he was meeting Docta restrained him. His action was so visible and funny that the others could not resist laughing out their lungs. The laughter brought temporary relaxation to the atmosphere that had been so far tensed ever since they embarked on the journey. Even Docta joined in the momentary jaw-muscle relaxation exercise.

The laughter was short-lived and did not however help Wiymanla to convalesce from the heavy load in his heart. As he sat in that shrine, the thoughts of his father's whereabouts queued up in his psyche like school children in the canteen ready for food. It once more dawned on him that they had come all the way from Kou to find out what had actually happened to Papa Wirayen. When Docta spoke, Wiymanla's reaction immediately betrayed that something serious was eating him up.

"Na weh we don laugh small, mi we go back for business. Weti I fi do for you?" Docta enquired, looking directly at Wiymanla.

Wiymanla thrust his head in between his hands and robbed his hair vigorously. He also rolled his palms to his face and robbed it before eventually resting them on his jaws. While in that position, he stared at Docta for a sometime and then said.

"Docta, I am troubled in body and spirit".

"No bi e concern your Papa? Docta said, partly interrogatively and partly informatively.

Wiymanla answered "Y-e-s" in a shriek voice and with a wondering face. He did not understand how Docta managed to know that the visit to the shrine concerned his father. Wiymanla had thought that Docta would behave like most witch doctors that began by finding out what was disturbing the visitor. But the man shocked him with his rhetorical question. He gazed at the man, trying to figure out how he managed to get it right so easily but there was no clue to that. Wiymanla turned and looked at Ba Ngwang suspiciously yet could not find any trace of guilt in the old man's wrinkled face. Ba Ngwang was busy chewing kola nuts and did not even realise that somebody was observing him. Docta looked at Wiymanla for some time and shook his head as he turned to collect *Fu* from the side. He soon emerged with a half calabash containing objects of all kinds. One or two beer covers, pieces of broken glasses, diamond, twisted pieces of zinc, cocks of blue and red pens, pieces of broken calabash, a wrapped piece of cloth and so many other objects were half full in the ancient calabash that had lost its original colour. Docta also collected a very small clay pot that stood near him and filled it with some dry-leaf concoction that he collected with his thumb and index from one of those numerous bags. He added a little quantity of incense into the pot. He lit a stick of match and dropped it inside the pot that flamed almost

55

immediately. He lifted the flaming clay pot up and passed it from left to right on top of *Fu* several times before putting it down somewhere around him. He held out the *Fu* to Wiymanla and asked him to place his hand on it and say what he wanted the gods to do for him. When this ritual was performed, Docta deliberately lifted the calabash up and down like a woman fanning out chaffs from threshed maize, allowing the different objects to fall back into the calabash disorderly. He did so three or four times then threw out all the objects unto a mat in front of him. Two objects in red rolled out violently from the mass and landed just in front of Wiymanla. Docta studied them keenly, shaking his head in the process. He gathered all the objects back into the calabash, performed the ritual again and threw them out once more. This time around, a different object still in red rolled out and landed in between Wiymanla's legs. Docta lifted his head, looked at Wiymanla for some time and then brought it down to the objects on the floor and enquired:

"Papa lost na since when?"

"E di come make four days…. Why you ask… and how you manage know?" Wiymanla stammered.

Docta issued a wry smile that faded out almost immediately and then said:

"For the place where your Papa dey, hmmm, I no sure say e still dey alive"

Wiymanla breathed out heavily like someone about to die. Two lines of sweat left his armpits and rolled down his shirt and he felt them dry off around his elbow. He tried to get up from his seat but his eyes were turning and he could not see clearly and his body was very weak, as if he had been sick for some time. He reclined and leaned against the wall until he regained his stamina. Nobody seemed to have been aware of what had happened to him. This was very surprising to him because he thought it was too obvious to go unnoticed. He perused the faces of all those present at Docta's shrine to see if someone was looking towards his direction. There was total silence and only exchange of looks animated the air. He wanted to protest against what Docta had just said but found no words nor courage to do so. Twice or thrice, he was pushed to ask Docta questions but hesitated as this urge was suppressed by an instinctive force that he himself could not understand. When his head had fully cleared up, he staggered to his feet and began walking away without a word. One by one, the others followed suit quietly like a congregation leaving the cemetery after the burial of a loved one. Docta got up and stood at the threshold of his shrine watching them walk away. He stood there still, reminiscent of an accused in the courtroom waiting for the presiding judge to dish out his sentence; his arms folded just slightly above his chest. His eyes followed them until they had faded out of sight.

When it was evident that they had gone for good, Docta walked round to the back side of his residence where he had planted different kinds of medicinal plants. He sent his hand across an overgrown *fever grass* and cut a thick leaf of *aloe vera plant* that stretched to the far end of the garden. He examined it closely, twisted it, threw it into his mouth and started chewing it gradually and carefully as if in an attempt not to hurt either his teeth or the plant. He kept a near smile look which somehow gave a deceptive impression that the *aloe vera* had an adorable taste. After barely two minutes of chewing and walking round, Docta swallowed the *aloe vera*. He threw the last glance round his vicinity to reassure himself that there was nobody coming and bent down to enter the house. While inside, he crossed to the other side of the shrine where *Ngem*, the famous two-hand iron instrument that occupied a strategic position in the shrine, was laying. Docta rarely played it. There was no stereo-typed situation that necessitated him to play it! He did it spontaneously.

Docta gave a faint smile as he remembered how he admired *Ngem* when he was still a teenager. He used to escape from work or even school whenever he heard that *Shigwaala* was out. We wanted just to stand and watch someone play *Ngem* because he knew each time this juju came out, that instrument would be played. The person in charge of playing it made sure that he singled out himself from the other members so that he would be conspicuous. Whenever *Shigwaala* displayed and paused on one spot to receive praises from on-lookers, the *Ngem* player tiptoed closer and played the instrument with all elegance that accompanied it. This drew a lot of praises from the crowd and at times Docta found it difficult to decipher whether the reaction from the crowd was caused by the display from *Shigwaala* or from the agile *Ngem* player. With his left hand, the man held the instrument closer to his chest and then used the stick on the right hand to hit it with a lot of dexterity. Docta could vividly remember those days as if it was yesterday! He felt disappointed whenever he realised that the *Shigwaala* that had to move with *Ngem* player had come out without one.

And so Docta took up the ancient *Ngem* that had been battered by age. He equally collected a worn-out stick which, seemingly, had suffered from some years of contact with the iron instrument each time he brought the two together in those rare moments. He bent towards the clay pot that stood in the middle of the shrine. The pot too looked ancient but very much intact than the *Ngem*. However, its seemingly subtle use and stationary position could justify why the clay pot was less worn-out. No one could be convinced that the *Ngem*, the stick and the clay pot were not inheritance of some kind because they looked older than their user. With care and gentility, Docta began playing *Ngem* murmuring in his mother tongue. It was essentially an incantation session during which he communicated and had communion with his ancestors. It was so skilfully done in a way that the playing of *Ngem* did not clash with the incantations. The playing somehow served as an interval between the talking and the silent moment. The ritual went on ceaselessly for roughly five minutes! He then placed the *Ngem* exactly where he had collected it, moved round, forming a small circle just centimetres away from the clay pot. When he had finished, he went to one corner of the shrine where there was a bamboo bed. He took off the bathing slippers and climbed onto the bed. Docta lay down facing the ceiling and few minutes later, he started snoring.

CHAPTER SEVEN

Dusk had already fallen when Ba Ngwang, Wiymanla and the rest returned from Docta's shrine. The delegation from Kou was obliged to spend the night in Membia. By 6: 30 am, the following morning, they took the first car that was to drop them at Nos before they would continue to Kou. It was a difficult journey as the distance apparently seemed longer than it was when they were going to Membia. The silence that reigned in their midst was one which gave the impression that three strangers who happened to find themselves together were heading to the same destination. It was very unusual of Wiymanla and the two others who had undertaken that discovery trip to Membia. When they left Kou for Membia the previous day, they conversed on diverse topics and did not allow themselves to be overweighed by the subject of their mission. But when Ba Ngwang suggested that they should visit a native doctor, thoughts of an unfavourable feedback gripped his mind and did not leave it all the way to the shrine. Wiymanla was struggling to figure out how he would take it if the native doctor declared that his father was dead. He fought in vain to be positive as his heartbeat underwent unjustified increase making it impossible for him to wave away the funny thought that had come to rest on his mind. And then Docta's heart breaking declarations struck him like the arrow from a bow thrust into an escaping soldier's back!

Docta's words were too heavy for Wiymanla's fragile look. He found it extremely difficult to overcome his emotions. The others were quick to realise that and decided to keep their calm. No discussion was initiated or even if one was, it died down as soon as possible. Wiymanla was deeply rooted in thoughts. The very idea that the villagers would bother him because he knew his people very well, kept haunting him. They were definitely going to accuse him in one way or the other in case Docta's declarations were valid. Even if they did not do that to his face, he was sure the slandering that he had killed his father would spread somehow. He also feared that the spirit of his father was not ever going to forgive him for not doing something immediately that night that Pa Wirayen left the hospital. He knew that it was quite late into the night and unsafe for someone who had spent his entire life in the village to walk away into the dark with that temperament! But he did nothing to prevent his father who knew virtually nothing about township and probably mistook it for the village setting. There in Kou, people kept late night as long as they could support the cold and were not scared by fairy tales about the passing of ghosts at certain hours of the night.

Wiymanla did not like the way his thoughts were going. He particularly hated the idea that he was looking for every argument to blame himself. What was he to do to prevent the imminent from happening? His father had left in anger because his wife had given birth to the fifth female child. Was he God to decide when to have a male child in order to satisfy his father's ego? He concluded with an unflinching conviction that he was a man and was ready to stand firm and not be swept away by what he almost had no control over. He searched for a bottle of water from his bag, lifted his head up like a fowl and sipped more than half of the content nonstop.

He breathed out heavily and turned to Kingum to ask for time. It had gone pass 8am and they were just arriving in Nos. When the car came to a halt and passengers were alighting, Wiymanla announced to the others that he had to stop at Nos Baptist Hospital to find out how his wife and the new-born were faring before continuing

The early hours of the day were exceptionally very busy ones for the personnel of the Nos Baptist Hospital because they had to carry out a variety of morning routine chores. The cleaners got to work at 5: 30am and by 6: 30am, they were done. Then, patients were asked to liberate the wards for the bed dressers to replace bed sheets and blankets of the previous day. Patients who were too weak were helped outside, supported on both sides by hospital attendants or pushed on wheelchairs. Since Nos was generally very cool especially in the morning, most patients had to bathe with warm water. At strategic positions of the hospitals, patients, or their caregivers, queued up, collected warm water and headed straight to the bathroom without wasting time. The number of bathrooms was not enough and so they needed to be fast and make way for others. Patients sometimes quarrelled over who had to go in first and this, at times, degenerated to a fight but the hospital security was always on alert to put an end to such unruly behaviour. Patients in very critical condition did not have to go through the ordeal. They were helped back to the wards once the bed dressing exercise was over and their caregivers collected water and bathed them on the spot. With the help of large tent-like barriers, the site was veiled and the patient bathed just beside his or her bed.

By 7:30am, patients took breakfast. Different kinds of food were always available at the hospital canteen at affordable prices. Those who did not have money simply went to the canteen and collected the food and it was included in their hospital bill to be settled when they were discharged. As soon as the clock struck 8 am, nurses, exclusively dressed in white gown began pushing in carts full of drugs, heading directly to their assigned patients. After a brief exchange with a patient, aimed at finding out how the patient was doing, the nurse served the patient and instructed him or her on the dosage of the drugs. Some of these nurses were so kind, soft spoken and encouraging that each time they passed by, patients confessed that they felt much better.

Amidst this atmosphere, Wiymanla arrived in the hospital premises. Full of eagerness, he walked past people to the maternity ward. The guard on duty could not allow him in because it was not yet visiting hours for the maternity section. He was acting on firm instructions from the hospital authorities who insisted that people should not be allowed in so early because doctors and nurses needed more time to attend to special cases like that of Wiymanla's wife. With premature births, it was always like that in Nos Baptist Hospital; not even relatives had free access! So, Wiymanla had to wait till 11: am. What could he do but loiter around the impressively vast premises, feeding his curious eyes with the marvellous infrastructures. The hospital was built on a hilly topography and it required a lot of ascending and descending to move from one end to another. The general landscape of the area was just like that! It was quite rare to come across a plain surface in Nos. As Wiymanla waited for the appointed time, he aimlessly strolled within the clean and flower-paved lawns admiring the beauty of the terrain. He visited the psychiatric section and stood at the window peeping at the people whose mental situation had gone out of hand. He was excited by the sight and tried on several occasions not to laugh out. At one point, he could not hold back himself when he saw one of the mentally deranged seriously advising his ward mates. It was reminiscent of a story his primary school teacher once told them. What was so peculiar about the story was not actually its realistic nature but the humour it carried. Right away, the plot began taking shape in his mind as he tried to connect the action in the ward to that in the story…

"When Gilbert found himself on the Chicago high way, he was over excited to come across a very wide road and with virtually no vehicle. He stepped up the accelerator of his vehicle and was cruising up the well tarred high-way at 200 km per hour. Soon he heard sirens after him. He became confused and instead stepped up the acceleration again and was now at 250km per hour. The police soon caught up with him and without a single word, they arrested and handcuffed him. Then they led him to the van and drove directly to a psychiatric hospital. Gilbert could not make any logical connection between where he was and where he was arrested. With his head down, he sat at the reception, wandering why they had brought him there in the first place. He had not stolen the car or anything; he was not an asylum seeker. What baffled him the more was that nobody was ready to talk to him. He had tried to enquire from the police what the problem was as they drove all the way to that place but all ignored him. Gilbert sat there waiting with his head completely buried in-between his legs. At one point, he lifted it up to check what was going on. Behold! The police were gone and all what he could see was a queue of madmen and women formed round him. Just in front of him, the doctor stood staring at him with a syringe in hand preparing to inject his arm. In a desperate attempt to make a point, he got up briskly, formed a fist and smacked the bench in front of him shouting:

"Can some-one tell me what is going on here? I am not mad"

To his greatest surprise, one of the mad men got up from the far end of the queue, came up to him and started advising him:

'My brother, take it easy. That is how it starts. Take it easy'.

Shocked, Gilbert prepared another fist, this time around with the two hands and hit the bench with his entire energy saying:

"I said I'm not M-A-D"

The madman came closer, held him by the collars and spoke in a soft voice that instead scared him:

"I asked you to take it easy my brother. This is how we all began. We thought it was a joke but it later on degenerated to something else. So take it easy..."

Suddenly, Wiymanla felt a heavy hand on his shoulder. He startled and then turned round gently like a criminal surrendered at gun point, asked to do whatever action he is commanded to do or else the trigger would be pulled at him. And indeed, it was the hospital security man who had tapped him. Without a word, he showed him the way out of the psychiatric section. Wiymanla hurried away with his toes barely touching the ground, constantly turning and looking behind to reassure himself that he was not being followed. When he was completely out of sight, he took to his heels until he reached the waiting room, panting like an antelope that had just narrowly escaped from the claws of a tiger. Those who were already there waiting for the visiting hour turned their eyes on him, half questioning, half wondering!

CHAPTER EIGHT

He sat on the bench just directly opposite the maternity room waiting. He could hear the cries of babies from the ward. The team comprising the doctor and nurses was attending to the new-borns. Mothers too were occupied suckling them, dressing them up or simply changing them. The atmosphere was indeed a busy one within the confines of the maternity ward. Wiymanla's heart leapt. He commenced developing strange feeling that he himself could not explain. The excitement that had characterised him when he first stepped foot into the hospital that morning began dwindling, giving way to horror and dismay. Many things he had virtually forgotten started clouding his mind again. He remembered that it was going to be the first time he would see the child since her birth; the birth that had caused the disappearance of his father; a disappearance that had become mystery! Who would have imagined that Papa Wirayen's simple gesture that night was to turn into something else? And now they had returned from Membia more confused!

Wiymanla battled between the ceaseless cries from the maternity ward and the old thoughts that were forming in his mind. The information from the witch doctor haunted him once more. What he had gathered from Docta's shrine somehow looked founded but he did not want to live by them. He wanted to keep on hoping and even believing that all was well with his father wherever he was! He did not want to think about anything in that light at that particular moment. He had come to see his wife and the new-born and this was certainly not the moment to spoil the show with imaginations of that nature. He kept on lifting up his eyes and resting them on the wall, until the shortest hand of the clock struck 11 am and the man on guard announced that it was time for visit. He was the first to get up and forge ahead as if in competition with others. He hurried into the maternity ward with anxious eyes that combed every bed of the place but could not see his wife and daughter in any of those beds. Looking very worried, he rushed to one of the hospital attendants he had pushed pass at the door without greeting and asked:

"Excuse me, have you seen my wife and daughter"

The man turned and looked at him, shook his head and said:

"Good morning sir. Even if we do not know each other, courtesy demands that when we meet someone for the first time we should greet".

Full of shame and guilt, Wiymanla responded down his throat with his head bent down. It was an embarrassment for someone to be reminding him of such basic tenets that were instinctive in everyone who grew up in that part of the country. He felt so bad that this type of uncultured behaviour had to come from him, and could not understand how he had failed to recall that greeting was the very first thing to exchange when people met. The man saw the guilt in him and felt sorry for him. He tapped Wiymanla by the shoulder severally and tried as much as possible to comfort him. This gesture was enough to step up his morale. He gave a faint and dry smile as he tried to enter a conversation with the hospital attendant. In the course of their discussion, Wiymanla explained the state of his wife and the conditions under which she gave birth. The man led him to the section where premature children and mothers were kept. They were separated from others because they needed special care.

From a distance, he could make his wife out. She also saw him and started off. They met at the centre of the ward and embraced each other passionately. Then she led her husband to where the baby was. Excited, he rushed to the site but immediately coiled back taking a sign of cross several times. He wiped his face too. Perspiration burst out from every part of his body. He went closer again, carried the child from the baby's cot and quietly sat down on the chair beside the main bed. He took in a long breath and began examining the baby carefully. Yes! His eyes had not deceived him! The baby was very fair in complexion, with eyes like those of a doll. The eyes kept on rotating each time she opened them. He noticed that she did not resemble him at all; instead, she was the complete picture of their neighbour in the village. Her ears, nose, mouth, eyes; in fact, virtually everything was that of Kilem. The only slight difference was in colour; Kilem was quite dark like most of the people from the northern part of the country. Wiymanla turned and looked at his wife, looked at the child again and could not find words to address her! Instantly, he left the ward and began walking away aimlessly. His wife called to him but he did not turn nor answer. His body was physically present there but his mind and spirit were elsewhere.

As he staggered down to the park, thoughts criss-crossed his mind in a zigzag manner. It was difficult, really difficult for

Wiymanla to come to terms with these successive happenings in his life. He tried to draw a logical connection between each event and the other but nothing seemed to work. The much-needed comfort and relief he thought he would find in Membia had not come his way. And now, to put more fuel into his already flaming heart, his wife had given birth to what he could not find words to describe! It hurt him to think about what he had just seen at Nos Baptist hospital. He walked down the tarred stretch of the road, ignoring the fast-running vehicles that kept on hooting behind him. What did they want him to do? Leave the pedestrian path for them? He hissed and shook his head simultaneously.

When he reached the motor park, it had gone past 2pm. The park boys saw him and rushed towards him in their numbers. One grabbed him by the left hand, the other by the right hand and two by his shirt, pulling him from one end to another, each claiming that he was their passenger. He did not even have the force to resist and like a child in the midst of two parents claiming right over him or her, he allowed them to drag him carelessly by both arms and shirt. He finally found a voice to announce his destination. This at least reduced the pressure on him as he was soon abandoned to the park boys responsible for vehicles loading for Kou. Two of them continued holding him and leading him like a hardened prisoner in the hands of security forces. They led him to the on-loading vehicle which was still empty. He was not happy to realise that he was the first passenger in that car because that meant he would spend at least three hours waiting for the car to be full. That was always the case when one had to travel to Kou on a none-market day. Passengers were very rare on such days.

He secured a seat beside the driver and sunk into it uncontrollably. It was then that he noticed the degree of hunger and tiredness in him. His intestines groaned and he constantly yawned carelessly, exposing his pre-molars and molars like a neighing horse. Since the break of the day he had not had a bite and now it was more than two hours after midday. After sojourning on the front seat, he dropped his bag there and walked into a nearby restaurant and ordered for rice and beans which was immediately served. Wiymanla made a sign of the cross, buried his face in his palms and prayed. As he lifted the first spoonful into his mouth, a cloud of endless thoughts began gathering in his mind once more. The fact that his father was missing could not let him be. He became frightened the more when he recalled what Docta said. He was still too worried about what might have happened to his father. Although his father was a mortal and could die like anybody, what disturbed him more were the circumstances, the mystery surrounding the whole issue! And then the latest from the hospital was a real blow that had brought him completely down on his knees. The birth of this very child had provoked his father's anger. The old man walked away that night and had not been seen again. A child that bore features of a different person! The villagers would certainly forge a connection between the two incidents to nail him down. Whatever link they would create, he did not know but he was quite sure they would do that! He knew them very well. They always found a way to heap the death of someone on another person's head. And once those people nurtured a thought, no one could make them wave it aside!

The rapidity with which the car got full that day surprised him a lot. Just slightly above an hour the vehicle was set. Everybody was already seated but for Wiymanla and one guy whom nobody knew their whereabouts. Wiymanla had not hoped to be long in the restaurant and so did not deem it necessary making his destination public. He was naturally a fast eater and was convinced that within five or so minutes he would be through. Even if he were to go beyond that, there was no cause for alarm because the vehicle was virtually empty when he paid. But after he was served, the appetite evaporated and he found himself rather plunged into a world of thoughts that neither seemed to have a logical beginning nor ending. For the past few days, events had taken a dramatic and inexplicable twist in his life that each time he had breathing space, thoughts overshadowed his brain like nimbus cloud usurping the sun in a dry season afternoon. He sat on top of the plate of rise completely carried away. People came and greeted him but he did not answer. He heard it like a dream. He felt crammed to thoughts that could not let him be. They would have thought him rude and would be right in thinking so because they did not know what he was going through! But the few who took time off to observe him immediately discerned from his gazing posture that something was definitely wrong with him. It was evident that he was physically present but his spirit was miles and miles away from him.

Drivers plying to or from Kou always wanted to take advantage of the least situation like good weather or the availability of passengers to be on the move because with the nature of the road, they were never sure to arrive their destination safely. The Nos-Kou road was indeed so bad that the virtually 25km stretch was charged at 15.00 FRS per passenger. During the rainy season, it was a nightmare and whenever it rained, no driver was ready to ply the road at whatever fare! They preferred to spend the night at Nos than to do so along the way, pushing the vehicle. There were areas along that road where only special vehicles with four-wheel drive could cross whenever it rained. Those places became very muddy and filled with water that the driver could not decipher which part of the road contained a safe track. At times, a vehicle pushed right to the top of the hill, would suddenly come back on reverse to the very spot where it got hooked. The road was so bad that be it in the dry or rainy season, it was useless for a passenger to dress up well. In the dry season, passengers were literally covered with dust at the end of the journey and in the rainy season they arrived their destination well rubbed with mud like a pig after basking itself in a pigsty.

CHAPTER NINE

The driver fumed with anger as he went from one drinking spot to another in search of the two missing passengers. He wanted to leave while places were still clear in order to control his movement along the road that was relatively new to him. It had been two weeks since he started plying that road but on that particular day, it would be the first time he was going to drive by night; something he feared so much because he had a very shallow knowledge of the road. The driver had even started contemplating on handing over the few passengers he had to an expert. He was therefore much relieved when the vehicle was fully loaded in the less than two hours. That meant if he left then, he would arrive before nightfall. Now, the two passengers not yet on board were making life very difficult for him.

After close to ten minutes of fruitless search, the driver walked into the restaurant in what he considered to be the last attempt. It was there that he stumbled on Wiymanla gazing at the plate of food right in front of him. He moved closer and tapped him violently on the shoulder shouting at the top of his voice that he had made him suffer. But when the young man lifted up his head, the driver noticed that Wiymanla's eyes were frighteningly red like those of someone who had been taking marijuana. A careless line of spittle too had rolled down his cheek and was now gently dropping into the plate in front of him. Immediately he noticed the presence of the driver, he quickly wiped his mouth with the back of his left hand looking guilty at every move he took. He did not even greet the driver who stood there mouth ajar, not knowing what to do. The driver watched every move of his with a lot of concern, his initial mood gradually fading away. At first there was apathy in the driver's look but this soon turned into pity.

The driver noticed that the man looked really tired and disturbed. From all indications, he wanted to eat but something was certainly bothering him beyond limit. The plate of food was still there the way it was served with some two heavy pieces of beef protruding from there. The driver leaked his salivating lips as if in expectation for someone to give him the go ahead to devour the delicious dish. Although the food was already cold, the aroma that issued from there could not leave someone indifferent. Wiymanla pushed the dish aside, stretched himself in a careless manner, feeling his pockets and moving towards the counter. He soon emerged with a 500frs coin which he handed to the man in charge of the restaurant. The driver followed every movement, divided over his loyalty to his sympathy for the man and the food that kept on reminding him that he was hungry. He looked round surreptitiously to see whether people were looking at him and noticed that nobody even had his time. He stretched his unwashed hand towards the plate and turned round once more to reassure himself that nobody was observing him. By the time he turned again to grasp the plate of food, it was gone. One of the servants in the restaurant had taken it and was heading with it where they washed dishes. The driver changed the direction of his hand and lifted it to cover his wide opened mouth. The yawning looked artificial and well calculated. He saw Wiymanla walking out. He too left his position and started following him from behind with his head down. Mid way from the door post, he lifted up his eyes which met with those of a customer who seemed to have been watching him from the beginning to the end. The man smiled at the driver who stealthily sneaked out of the place without returning what was meant to be mutual.

The journey was particularly tedious for Wiymanla. Even though it looked like the shortest journey he had ever undertaken on the rough road, his mind was completely eclipsed with ideas that did not give him any breathing space. The more they advanced, the more his psyche was subjected to trauma. He wondered what information he was going to give his people who were waiting for his return with a lot of expectation. His companions to Membia were already back at Kou but they were not the principal actors; everything rested on his shoulders! And then the birth of the fifth female child which was already being taken with a pinch of salt had another development.

In Kou, if a man gave birth to only female children, it meant he was not man enough, he was a weakling. He had tried to console himself that a child was a child; whether male or female because they all came from God and intended using the baby as a comfort at the time when the disappearance of his father was weighing so much on him. But then, what he just saw in the hospital shocked and demoralised him completely. His problem was not only that the child did not resemble him. He was the more worried over the fact that she was the carbon copy of his immediate neighbour. He could not understand how a child who was supposed to be his would instead bear features of another man who had no blood link to his family. He had never suspected his wife of infidelity, even once but this incident brought a lot of division in his head. He began having strong feelings that his wife had been deceiving him all this while. In his mind-set, he examined all his children and one thing kept on recurring; none of them actually resembled him. They all resembled their mother. All this while, he was convinced that it was so because they were female children but the fact that the last child looked exactly like his neighbour to have a rethink. So many questions were in his mind begging for answers that he could not provide! How was he to combine information from Docta and that from the hospital to give those villagers? These sagas gave him persistent frontal headache that held him spellbound throughout the journey!

The vehicle eventually came to a final halt at Kou Main Park. There was a general atmosphere of relief for the passengers who had remained packed inside the vehicle like slaves on transit from one coastal area to the other. While waiting for the car to be offloaded, they stretched their legs and arms in an uncoordinated manner. The legs were the most affected with majority suffering from muscle cramps. For those who were used to this type of journey, they were less worried. Among the seriously affected was a civil servant who had just been posted to Kou. He had travelled all the way from the capital of the Republic where he was born and bred. This had been a very tough undertaking for him covering over 300 km to where he now stood gazing at places as a stranger in a strange land. He immediately limped to a nearby broken bench and sat on it. The cramp in his legs could not allow him stand even for a minute. From his facial expression, it could be seen that he was in agony. He was certainly cursing the government that sent him to that remote area. He could not openly express his discontent for fear that the villagers might begin to detest him. Wiymanla stood for a while observing the young man in difficulty and shook his head in pity. He would have loved to comfort the fellow and embark on a discussion with him as a mark of hospitality but he was not in the mood for that. He collected his small traveller's bag and commenced covering the three kilometre walk to their compound.

Glimpses of nightfall were already visible almost everywhere in Kou. Wiymanla met with a good number of people going his way. They greeted him with very unusual solemnity and seriousness that scared him. How could people who used to greet him with camaraderie suddenly become so unnecessarily formal? And then, he noticed that they were wearing sad faces. Some of them, especially women, were even shedding tears! This immediately registered something in his mind. Someone was dead. He hurried home wondering who the deceased was! As he approached their compound, he started hearing something which first sounded like a hum. The closer he got, the louder and clearer it became. The humming was mixed with yelling. His blood ran chill and his heart thumped faster than before as he stepped into the compound. The first person he perceived from that distance was his mother sitting on the ground just at the entrance to the door. She was held on both sides by three or so women. She was struggling to free herself from their grip but did not have enough force to overpower those who held her down. When she saw Wiymanla, she tried to say something but was stuck. She seemed to have lost her voice. But from the gestures, Wiymanla could discern that the deceased was a close family member. He hurried into the parlour jammed full with family members and sympathisers. There was no space to sit but as soon as they saw him someone surrendered his seat instantly and walked out. He did not have the zeal to sit down. He by passed everybody on his way without a word and made his way into the inner chamber. No corpse was there. He rushed into another room and still found nothing. With prying eyes searching for answers to unasked questions, he moved towards his uncle whom he had neglected on his arrival. He saw him approaching and knew what exactly he wanted. He held Wiymanla by the hand and walked him out of the crowd to the backside of the compound. There, the whole mystery was unveiled to him.

CHAPTER TEN

Although Wiymanla was so disappointed that his father was buried in his absence, he somehow agreed with his uncle that that was the best thing to do. A hunter saw the remains of his father and immediately alerted the villagers who stormed the site in their numbers to see for themselves the very first death of that nature in Kou. Papa Wirayen had been chopped into pieces, put inside a bag and then dumped at the boundary between Kou and Nos. His sex organs were nowhere to be found. It was indeed a horrible sight and everything pointed to ritual killing. The land had been desecrated and the villagers watched the scene tongue tied and benumbed! Never had such a thing ever happened in Kou! They wondered what had to be done to appease the gods, to cleanse the land!

For days and even weeks, the death of Papa Wirayen made news in the entire clan. The people of Kou were particularly touched because it concerned a son of the soil. Everybody was calling for revenge. They wanted to fetch out the perpetrators of this gruesome act and deal with them accordingly. One clue at the site of the macabre scene guided them in the hunt for the manhunt. The national identity card of a certain Lohntum Barnabas was found where the bag with the corpse of Papa Wirayen was deposited. The bearer was born in Shimsong Hospital in Nos. Even the name and those of his parents all pointed to the fact that he was from Nos. One of the villagers picked it up and marked it as the leading and most reliable evidence. They did not need any further clue to conclude that the macabre act was carried out by people from Nos. Instantly, tempers began to flare at the spot. People, especially the youth were demanding for an immediate reaction. It was unanimously accepted that what had happened was an open provocation. The people of Nos had stretched it beyond limit and the only response was to strike back without any waste of time. A delegation was immediately dispatched to the palace to inform His Royal Highness about what had happened. The rest of the population followed the remains to the family compound where Papa Wirayen had to be inhumed.

In the compound, a serious dispute erupted as to where the corpse had to be buried. Papa Wirayen had been a fervent Catholic Church Christian for some years. But when his wife was involved in a sexual scandal with the parish priest, it pushed him into backsliding. Since then, it had been barely twenty years and he had not stepped foot in the church yard. He had devoted much of his time to his retailing business at the market square. He also became very involved in the activities of traditional groups like *Njong, Mfuh, Manjong* and *Ngiri*. The meeting days of these groups were already instinctive to him. He was always delighted whenever he found himself in those circles where he could dance, drink and discuss with people of his age group with the same mentality and perception of life.

And so, when the corpse reached the deceased compound, Christians and traditionalists were divided. The church people insisted that they had the right over the corpse of their faithful and as such he had to be buried in the church cemetery; a place reserved for Christians of the Catholic Church who were regular in the institution, led an exemplary life and were up to

81

date with their financial obligations. Even if a Christian died and had not fulfilled his or her financial dues, it was still possible for the person to be buried there on condition that his family was ready to update the financial contribution book of the deceased. In the case of Papa Wirayen, it had been virtually twenty years since he left the church. His financial track records were not easy to trace. Apart from his baptism card, nobody could lay hands on any church document that identified him. The local priest did not see that as a problem. He explained to Mama Wirayen that the essential thing was the baptism card which identified the deceased to the catholic faith. The family only needed to pay the financial contribution due the church and Papa Wirayen would be given a place in the mission burial ground.

Even with the priest's suggestion, there was still a slight hitch somewhere. Papa Wirayen's financial record with the church could not be traced given that it had been quite long since he withdrew from the church. Besides, there was no document showing when he last paid the yearly contribution. Again, that was not a serious issue to the priest. He simply estimated an amount which he thought could be at the reach of the family and asked them to pay. Mama Wirayen went home and called for an impromptu contribution from the family members and other well-wishers. She moved from door to door asking for financial support. None catholic Christians refused to take part in the contribution. The traditionalists too did not participate. Even at that, the amount went up to 20.000 frs CFA. She returned to the parish and handed it to the priest. When the man of God learned of the amount, he gave a faint smile. Without any further argument, he promised to conduct mass and other church rituals for the departed before his remains would be laid to rest in the church cemetery. Mama Wirayen went home certain that her husband's remains would be interred in the church burial ground. She had fought so hard for that and was happy that it was working. This was going to give her more grounds in the church and bring shame to those who mocked her when her late husband suspended his activities with the church.

Back in the family compound it was a different story. Staunch traditionalists, led by Wiymanla's uncle, stood their grounds. They swore that there was no way that the corpse would leave the compound to the church, talk less of the cemetery. Their colleague had to be buried where they would have free access to communion with him traditionally. They also added that taking him to where they considered a place meant for children was not dignifying. The late man was a family head with a compound and deserved to be buried where he would continue to monitor the daily activities of his home. He had to be kept closer to the ancestors because he was now one. To them, there was no other place fit for such a person than his compound. The traditionalists also said they did not want the spirit of their friend to get angry with them for allowing such a thing to happen. Anything contrary to what they wanted was a heavy blow to tradition and they were ready to fight against it till the last drop of their blood.

The fight between staunch traditionalists and fervent Catholic christians divided the people of Kou more than ever before. The argument soon took another dimension. It had moved from a mere disagreement to one that began to develop enmity among the people. Others even took it as a forum to settle their differences and were pouring out insults without control. This eventually reached the ears of His Royal Highness. He frowned at this attitude expressing disappointment at his people who could not show respect for the dead; a decomposing corpse for that matter! He ordered for an unconditional end to the squabble and instructed that Papa Wirayen's remains be inhumed within the next two hours in the courtyard of his compound. Mama Wirayen immediately rushed to the parish and informed the priest about the latest development. He thought for a while. He did not see himself engaging in a fight over a corpse with the people of the land. If they had decided to bury the man the traditional way he had nothing to do. The man of God collected the Rosary, Bible, Holy water and a small cross and followed Mama Wirayen to the compound. There, he prayed over the corpse with those who were interested and sprinkled Holy water on the coffin, around the compound and in the grave and left before traditional rites were carried out.

For barely three hours Kou vibrated to the rhythm of burial songs. Youth danced in ecstasy and with dexterity on top of the deceased tomb. It was a physical dance of six persons at a time. They danced following instructions from a leader who stood outside the grave blowing a whistle. Among the six in the grave, there was one person in charge of tuning and changing the song whenever he deemed it necessary. The others had the obligation to sing the chorus. After approximately every ten minutes, the dancing stopped and the dancers came out for more soil to be heaped into the tomb before they regained their positions inside. A dancer was changed immediately the leader judged that someone was no longer performant and entertaining enough. It was a real display of style in a choreographic manner that went on till the tomb was full. Some people departed as soon as the coffin was lowered into the grave while others waited till everything was over.

CHAPTER ELEVEN

The people of Kou did not want to waste time. They wanted to 'strike the iron while it was still hot'. His Royal Highness was taking a longer time to give the go ahead. He was adopting a diplomatic approach to the matter. His people were not happy with this. They kept on mounting pressure on him but that did not accelerate things either. The youth decided to take control of the situation. Just a day after the burial, they went on rampage in the early hours of the day and massacred anybody from Nos in Kou land that they came across. When the people of Nos heard about this, they went to action instantly. This rapidly degenerated into an inter-tribal war which lasted barely for a few days and left many casualties. Lives were lost and countless properties damaged.

In accordance with tradition, the people of Kou had to observe three days of mourning for Papa Wirayen after the burial. He was an elderly person and deserved to be mourned. He was also a man of the people, very popular within and without the land. They had to carry out the old-aged tradition so that his spirit that was still wandering around, asking for vengeance, should be laid to rest definitively. There were some routine post burial rites that had to be performed for a man of his calibre. He had also died under awful circumstances and some sacrifices had to be carried out to cleanse the land and appease the gods. The people of Kou lived by it and saw the work of the gods in virtually every good and bad happening in the land. Whenever there was low harvest, mysterious death, and absence of rain for a long time during rainy season or thunder destruction in the land, it was interpreted as a manifestation of the gods' wrath. They did not also fail to attribute great harvest and other positive occurrences in the land to the same gods.

Two months after the war, the people of Kou were very excited to learn that three days of mourning were set aside for Papa Wirayen. They saw this as an opportunity to give their late father a well-deserved farewell. His Royal Highness called on everybody to support in whatever way possible to make the occasion a success. He reminded them that the late man was not just a staunch traditionalist but was also a sociable man who, despite his strong affiliation to culture, remained flexible and ready to embrace Western ideas that could better the living condition of his people. He gave a cow, two goats and ten fowls to the family as royal assistance. Female relatives and some villagers also supported with food items like corn, beans, and vegetables. The men brought essentially palm wine, fowls and goats.

Papa Wirayen was a pillar in his family, always there, running up and down to keep the family going. Nobody seemed to notice or even feel that when he was alive. Now that he was gone, everybody felt his absence almost in every sphere as they prepared for the three-day mourning. He would have been the one at the forefront of virtually every organisation, tirelessly giving instructions and making sure that they were followed to the letter. His death was indeed a great loss not only to the family but to Kou as a whole! Wiymanla had to step up and embrace responsibilities he had not anticipated. He had really worked hard to keep himself at the right frame of mind during this phase of the ceremony. This could be seen and felt throughout the preparation but it was never to be like that of his late father.

On the eve of the actual celebration *Ruum* and *Kikumkevitseh* were there for animation. These are jujus that came out exclusively in the night and one had to be initiated before he could see them. The initiation was exclusively reserved for men who were discreet enough; men who could not be lured by non-members or women to unveil what usually happened in those *ngumba* houses. No woman, irrespective of her social status was allowed to be part of either *Ruum* or *Kikumkevitseh*. It was believed that if a non-member peeped, he was doomed for mysterious death or madness unless thorough cleansing was carried out. The person had to bring a goat, a white cock, a black hen and a jug of palm wine to the members for his official cleansing and initiation into the house. It became worse and even disastrous for a female outsider. She was immediately struck with madness and barrenness. If she was pregnant, she would have miscarriage or would labour for one week and eventually give birth to any of the jujus she saw. The present generation of Kou had grown up to meet this belief. Although none of them had seen it happen, the elderly told them that it was real. For fear of the unknown, those who did not belong to these juju houses simply steered clear, especially women, to avoid the curse.

That evening, many young guys were initiated into *Ruum* in late Papa Wirayen's compound. Initiation into *Ruum* was unique and quite demanding than into *Kikumkevitseh*. The initiators carried the newcomers on their shoulders to the base. Their eyes had to be firmly closed till the end of the initiation, lest they received the wrath of the gods. Once they were brought in, they were pinched and beaten carelessly by older members. This was what everyone who had to be initiated went through. Most young boys took this as an opportunity to avenge the beating and pinching they once endured during their own initiation. Wiymanla was particularly pleased to be part of it that evening. He had been waiting for this occasion for two years because ever since he was initiated, he had never had the chance to be part of an initiation ceremony. He was initiated at a very advanced age and many younger ones took the opportunity to deal with him. They tortured him up to the point that he wailed like a woman. He ran outside shouting for rescue but was immediately caught and brought back to the place. That day, he went home with swells and wounds all over his body.

The two young boys who had to be initiated were physically strong. Members were also excited to see such newcomers because they would not discourage them with a womanish cry. They were immediately welcomed at the entrance and brought down from the shoulders of the carriers to the ground by the older members. Wiymanla was the first to skip from his seat and land on one of them. He pounced on his shoulders and pinched him on the face with all the excitement. The boy struggled on the floor kicking at every direction like a cow in the hands of butchers but uttered no word. He had been made to understand that if he tried to resist, he would not be initiated. With others, Wiymanla rough handled the two new comers until the eldest person of the *Ngumba house* brought it to a halt.

The three-day mourning for Papa Wirayen was a crowd puller. Villagers came out in their numbers from the nooks and crannies of Kou and even beyond. It had been indeed long since a death celebration in Kou brought together such a mammoth crowd. Sheds were built all over the compound and were used to shield visitors from the dry season sun that had taken control of the climate and shone with immeasurable intensity. People ate and drank to satisfaction because there was enough food and alcohol. Mama Wirayen made sure that those in charge of cooking food were permanently at work so as to avoid shortage. The women in that group were visibly happy and satisfied the way things went on. They were not under too much control. Besides, they had a lot of advantages because of the laxity exercised by Mama Wirayen who was up and down welcoming new arrivals and making sure there was supply of food to strategic quarters. They therefore took advantage of any slight opportunity to select heavy pieces of meat, put them inside their *should in case* plastic bags and slid them into their handbags. In the evening they returned home with handbags full to the brim.

Things were organised in such a way that possible major hitches were limited. Apart from *Ruum* and *Kikumkevitseh* that lodged in the compound till the end of the ceremony, every other group returned to its original base in the evening and resurfaced the following day. The entire night was animated by the two stationed *Ngumba* houses and during the day, they went to rest giving way for the rest to take over. Turn by turn, each traditional group first went and danced on top of the grave before occupying their designated site where they spent the rest of the day entertaining the public.

Whenever they were tired of dancing, they halted and drank or ate. At some moments, food was not available but palm wine was always in excess. Men came with traditional cups in their bags and were always on alert. As soon as someone got up to share palm wine, they quickly searched for the cups from their bags as if in competition with one another and probably afraid the palm wine would get finished if one was not smart enough in bringing out the cup. Those who came without cups had to wait until someone felt full and decided to surrender his cup for some time. At times they waited in vain or had access to the cup when only the dregs of palm wine were left. In such cases, they had to keep their disappointment to themselves because they knew very well that a real man in Kou always went to an occasion with a traditional cup.

CHAPTER TWELVE

Although the government intervened and quelled the tribal war, the relationship between the three tribes remained one of tension and suspicion. The premature end to the war did not really bring a lasting solution to the power struggle between Nos, Membia and Kou. The people of each ethnic group tried at all cost to defend the interest of their own land. The people of Nos in particular kept on insisting that they were above those of Membia and Kou and there was no compromise to that. On their part, the people of Membia and Kou categorically refused to be regarded as inferiors. They maintained that they were all children from the same ancestral origin and had to be considered as equals. That meant that among their leaders, there was neither a paramount Fon nor a second class Fon. They were all colleagues in the first place and paramount only to those sub-chiefs in their respective ethnic groups.

The tussle for power between the three leaders made life unbearable for their people. There was no more guarantee of security and living together was in perpetual fear because anything could happen at any time. The atmosphere was so tense and it was imminent that another tribal war was around the corner if nothing was done to calm down tempers. The gods of the lands were consulted but they refused to speak. All attempts to make the Fons of Nos, Membia and Kou to come to a compromise ended in a stalemate because each of them claimed supremacy over the others. First of all, they could not agree on the meeting ground to sort their differences. The Fon of Membia wanted a meeting in his own palace because he claimed that traditionally, Membia was sanctioned by the gods. The Fon of Kou on his part did not see it customarily sound to leave his palace for a meeting in one of his wives' village. As for the Fon of Nos, there was nothing that could convince him to go out of his palace; be it to Membia or Kou. He remained the paramount ruler of the land and courtesy demanded that Mohammed should move to the mountain and not the other way round. None of the three leaders was ready to lose his pride for whatever reason. They were not prepared to let the logic of reason override their egos. Whether their individual reasons for wanting to host the crisis meeting were convincing or not, they were not interested in that. What mattered was the tussle for supremacy.

It therefore became an uphill task for the people of Nos, Membia and Kou to come out of the crisis plaguing the land. The sons and daughters of the land, especially those in the diaspora, came together to find a solution to the problem. After a series of meetings and failed attempts to bring the three leaders together, they decided to look for a judicial solution to the problem. They wanted to end the crisis by whatever means. Since the matter was between neighbouring ethnic groups within the same division, it could be handled within a local court. But the problem resurfaced as to which local court was competent enough to handle the problem without bias. Normally, the local court in Nos was the most qualified because it was the only one at the divisional level in the entire area. It was therefore unanimously agreed that the Nos local court should be the venue. The Fon of Membia and that of

Kou saw this as another turn around to let their colleague be seen as supreme to them. They therefore began questioning the integrity of those who took the matter to court and even that of the judge as well as his collaborators. Despite promises that the people to handle the issue would be brought from elsewhere; the two Fons maintained that it was a ploy put in place by the Fon of Nos to twist judgement in his favour. They swore that it was over their dead bodies that they would step their feet into that court.

Following the stalemate, no immediate solution could be envisaged. For weeks and eventually months, the tension between the three leaders remained unshakable. Joint sacrifices that had to be carried out by these leaders to keep the clan intact could no longer be executed because none of the three Fons wanted to take the first move and be seen as a weakling. The venue for these joint sacrifices was rotational and that year it had to be in Membia. The Fon of Kou was ready to travel to Membia with his delegation. The crisis between the three counterparts had not really affected the relationship between the two leaders. Besides, the two Fons were in-laws and the Fon of Membia had even come to rescue his colleague when the people of Nos attacked Kou. But then, how could the two of them effectively carry out the sacrifice without their counterpart? It was not that the Fon of Nos had something special to bring to the sacrifice but tradition demanded that the three of them come together for the gods to accept it. All of them were indispensable. Even if one of them could not be present, there had to be a genuine reason for that. By the way, apart from ill-health, no other reason was considered genuine and acceptable by the gods. In that case, a representative had to be chosen by the gods themselves.

On the 7th day after the deadline for the sacrifice, the Fon of Nos got up the following morning quite excited. Full of royalty and self esteem, he prepared for the day and stationed himself on the throne ready to receive visitors. It was a routine exercise and he enjoyed it very much. Each time someone entered the palace and stooped before him to perform the royal obligations before sitting down, His Royal Highness was very happy. Without uttering a word, and with a broad smile that accomplished his sumptuous appearance, he nodded when an elder or a youth, qualified to greet the Fon mechanically carried out greeting rituals before him. And so, that morning, the Fon had just taken his seat outside the palace courtyard. The closest servant was heading to announce to the general public that they could now pay a royal visit when he heard a loud and agonic shout:

"Gwey, where are you... where are you? I cannot see... I cannot see". The wailing came from His Royal Highness on his feet struggling to move in every direction but none in particular.

"Please help me inside... I cannot see". He continued yelling. Gwey hurried back and held his hand. He passed his hand from left to right just in front of the Fon's face to verify whether he could notice the movement but His Royal Highness remained indifferent.

It was actually true that the supreme ruler of the people of Nos had gone completely blind. Those who were outside waiting to be ushered in heard the cry and were curious to know what had happened. They all bumped into the palace and caught the last glimpse of their leader as he was being helped into the inner chambers. They did not need to be told what had happened because he kept on shouting that he could not see. Besides, his movement betrayed him. It was typical of someone who was living his first days or even hours in a blind state. Yes, it was really true that His Royal Highness could not see again. Never had that ever happened in the land. Never! Word instantly went round that what had happened should remain within the confines of the palace. He was immediately rushed to a special hospital out of the land.

Except His Royal Highness had travelled or was sick, it was unthinkable that one week passed by without him making a public appearance. When two weeks elapsed, his absence increasingly became a public concern. The people were further disturbed when the cultural week that was usually presided over by their Fon came and passed and nothing was heard of him. This started raising a lot of eyebrows and the truth could no longer be hidden. The mysterious blindness that had struck the palace soon became a sing-song even by children who did not even know what it all meant. After a few weeks in the emergency ward in a hospital at the nation's capital, it was declared that His Royal Highness could never see again. He had to temporarily abdicate the throne to seek medical solution abroad. The elders of Nos came together and unanimously accepted that while waiting for the condition of His Highness to ameliorate, the royal activities of the land had to move on. The eldest notable of the land was chosen to occupy the royal throne and lead the people of Nos for the time being.

News of the misfortune that had befallen the Nos fondom spread like wildfire. The more it disseminated the more it was modified and the real truth was completely thwarted. Even people who were not present when it happened told the story like eyewitnesses. Some claimed that the Fon of Nos had lost his sight and had fled to the Whiteman's land. In Membia and Kou, the news was received with mixed feelings. Some were happy while others were not. The Fon of Membia and that of Kou were quite elated and showed no pity for their colleague. They saw the misfortune that had struck their colleague as a victory for them. He had been a thorn in their flesh, an aching tooth. Few days after, His Royal Highness, the Fon of Membia dispatched an envoy to Kou asking his colleague to come over so that they could carry out the delayed sacrifice. Since the aching tooth had been removed, the mouth could then chew comfortably. He also sent words to the temporary ruler of Nos to join them.

On the day of the sacrifice, all the traditional rulers in Membia were present. Even those that were already much advanced in age had to defy nature and remain standing throughout the exercise. Everyone stood according to his status in the traditional cycle. The two Fons as well as that of Nos were at the centre stage of activities. They were the ones vested with traditional authority to lead in that very demanding and implicating sacrifice. Once everything was set, the Fon of Membia held out a traditional cup into which palm wine was filled to the brim. On both hands, the Fon of Kou carried a healthy-looking white fowl while the ruler of Nos, in like manner, stood with a black cock.

"Ah a nyuy ver…" the Fon of Membia began talking and simultaneously pouring wine into the ground. "We have gathered here today to offer our annual and routine sacrifice to you…" He looked up at his two colleagues and other traditional rulers standing round him. All of a sudden, The Fon of Kou let go of the fowl he was holding and was seriously shaking his head with each of the two index fingers forced into his two ears. After few minutes of seemingly fruitless struggle, he removed the index fingers and instead blocked the ears with his palms. His action was so prominent that nobody could be indifferent. Confused, they all moved towards him, with curious looks, mesmerised by his gesticulations. Everybody was trying to find out at the same time what the matter was. The man himself seemed the most embarrassed as he started moving in every direction shouting:

"Somebody help… gods of my ancestors… I cannot hear…somebody help"! The Fon of Membia let loose his hand and the traditional cup fell to the ground spilling its content. He rushed to his colleague struggling to gather the shoulders and in-between the laps his traditional regalia that came trailing on the ground. He tried to talk to the already raging Fon of Kou but no word was issued out from his mouth. He insisted and noticed that he had become tongue-tied. Scandalised, he made the last frantic effort yet nothing worked. Without much ado, the temporary ruler of Nos flung the cock he was carrying and took to his heels. The rest followed almost immediately. Even elderly traditional rulers, whose age had "handicapped" them from certain physical and energy consuming exercise, took off too. The two Fons also came running after them with the Fon of Kou shouting for help and that of Membia only gesticulating.

CHAPTER THIRTEEN

News of the twin mishaps that just visited the clan left nobody indifferent. Fear gripped the sons and daughters of Membia and Kou alike as they found it extremely difficult to come to terms with the bitter reality. Those who were not there when it happened listened in disbelief to eyewitness account of the horrifying incident. The general atmosphere was that of uncertainty. If Fons could fall prey to the wrath of the gods, it meant anybody was vulnerable and could be hit at anytime. The people of Nos, Membia and Kou were further plunged into confusion when few days later the Fon of Nos was brought back to the land in the same condition as he had left. He was still unable to see despite the time spent with different eye specialists abroad and had therefore been declared visually impaired for life.

With the three Fons down, it became clear that something was definitely wrong which had provoked that wrath of the gods. Nos, Membia and Kou were now like fondoms without real rulers and were temporarily managed by auxiliaries. Since a Fon could not be replaced in his lifetime or allowed to rule in bad shape, the custodians of the land thought it wise to put in place auxiliaries. They had to see into the day to day running of the fondoms as the villagers mobilised in search of the root cause of the strides that had brought the clan to its knees. It was no longer a Nos, Membia or Kou affair but a collective problem of the descendants of Tikak. For the first time in decades, people of the three fondoms had to bury their differences and go to the drawing board in one spirit to trace where "the rain started beating them".

All the powerful custodians of tradition of the land were mobilised to harness their opinion on what should be done to save the clan. It was no longer a matter of where a suggestion was coming from, but the question of what idea could lead the people out of the crisis. And so when the custodians of tradition met, they came to a consensus that the presence of the ailing Fons in the land was preventing the gods from communicating to lead them out of the undesirable situation. They were transferred to the outskirts where they lived together under the custody of a renowned witch doctor. That same night, the gods spoke to Ba Ngwang and instructed him to form a six-man commission that had to carry out consecrating activities at some key spots in the land. He was to be their spiritual leader.

A commission made of representatives from the three ethnic groups was immediately put in place. It comprised essentially of elderly people versed with the tradition and the history of the clan and was led by the three auxiliary rulers. For three days, they concerted with each of three fondoms paying secret visits to some sacred and reserved places of the land. At about midnight of the last day, they met in the sacred fountain situated at the site where Nos, Membia and Kou first settled. There, some rituals were performed till the early hours of the following day.

After three days of consecration, the gods again spoke to Ba Ngwang and gave him further directives. There and then he could see clearly the root cause of the problems in the land.

The three Fons had desecrated the land with their egos and had neglected some sacrifices for so long. This had provoked the wrath of the gods and the only way out was for the same Fons to be led on a great trek back to Nkim where the people of Nos, Membia and Kou first settled. There, they had to be initiated back to the right track by the supreme ruler of Nkim. He was the oldest human being in the entire clan and was part of the great trek undertaken by the descendants of Tikak clan close to a century ago. Although he was now very old, he still remembered the history of the clan as if it happened yesterday. The supreme ruler of Nkim was like a father to the Fons of the warring tribes. In the past, he used to be consulted whenever there was a misunderstanding between Nos, Membia and Kou. Ever since the present leaders took over, he had been completely forgotten.

The journey to Nkim was quite a long one and many people wanted the kick-off to be early enough so that they should arrive before dusk. Everybody who wished to be part of the great trek was present at the sacred fountain on time. At the first cockcrow, Pa Ngwang ordered for the historic trek to commence. The Fon of Nos refused to move saying that the timing was biased. He was supported by the delegation from his land which insisted that even if their Fon could not see, he should at least be given the privilege to feel his way when places were clear. This was immediately heeded without debate. The delegation of roughly fifty persons had to wait at the fountain till 6 am when they set out for Nkim. Supported on both sides by able bodied young guys, the visually impaired Fon of Nos forged on. He sometimes stumbled as he struggled to feel his way but was motivated to get back to his feet almost immediately by the entourage. Right beside him to his right-hand side was the Fon of Membia who had all this while, not found a way to lay his grievances. He was not very satisfied with the pace that occasionally forced him to move like someone divided between running and walking. Each time he felt it was too much for him to bear, he dragged the closest person by the cloth or simply slapped. Such reactions somehow relieved the Fon of Kou who was constantly nervous throughout the journey because he was lost in the discussion that animated the group. Each time people laughed out, he interpreted it as a mockery directed towards him since he could not hear.

It was indeed a demanding journey meant for men and not for boys. They defied the hot whether up the hills and down the valleys. Whenever they felt too exhausted, they rested and replenished their energy with palm wine and kola nuts. By the time they crossed the boundary to Nkim more than half of the population had given up along the way. The excitement with which the group started off the journey died down completely and there was no sign of its resurrection. The three Fons staggered on, almost on their knees. It was not long before Ba Ngwang announced that they had entered Nkim land. But they still had approximately three kilometres to be in the fiefdom of the supreme ruler of the land. Suddenly the Fon of Kou cried out:

"I can hear people. My ancestors I c-a-n h-e-a-r…"

Everybody was startled by such an unexpected announcement. They crowded round him like bees on a hive, mouths wide open. Then another shout came from the Fon of

Membia who started babbling out sensible words whose meanings were overshadowed by the stammer in his voice. Almost simultaneously, the Fon of Nos broke loose from the youth who had been leading him all through and was raving at the top of his voice. He was regaining his sight. The hearing was not perfect, the talking was not the best, the seeing was not sharp but all these were signs of light at the end of the tunnel. Life started coming back to the group that had been literally dead. With revived spirit and renewed determination, the crew cruised to Nkim. The supreme ruler of Nkim saw them at a distance as they approached his fiefdom. He went to the shrine in front of his compound and began evoking the spirits of the ancestors. His incantations were characterised by proverbs meant for the elitists of Tikak language....

www.ingramcontent.com/pod-product-compliance
Lightning Source LLC
Chambersburg PA
CBHW051307170626
46809CB00004B/1793